LITTLE TURNCOAT

BOOK 6 - PATRIOT KIDS OF THE AMERICAN REVOLUTION

GEOFF BAGGETT

Cocked Hat Publishing

DEDICATION

This book is for the amazing Garrison kids of South Carolina. They come to visit me at almost every Colonial event I attend in that state. It was their sincere encouragement that compelled me to get back to writing and finish this book. I hope they are pleased with the story.

PART I

WE SERVE THE KING

1

JACKSON'S CREEK

The South Carolina Backcountry
September 25, 1775

It was mid-afternoon, the very hottest part of the day. William Newman, age eleven, suffered terribly in the scorching South Carolina heat. He craved some cooling shade, if only for a short while. He closed his eyes and prayed desperately for a cloud that might temporarily cover the blazing-hot sun. Then, his prayer completed, he opened his eyes and peered expectantly upward. His heart sank. There was not a cloud to be seen in any direction. Except for the glowing, yellow-orange sun, the sky above him was a deep, clear azure blue.

"A breeze would surely be nice," William muttered out loud to himself. He cast a quick glance at the tall oak trees that lined the western edge of his father's cornfield. Again, he was disappointed. The leaves of every tree dangled limply on their branches and remained absolutely still. There was not the slightest hint of any wind. It was hopeless. There was no escape from the unbearable heat.

The exhausted lad's lungs ached for just one breath of cool, refreshing air. But, in South Carolina in September, the simple act of breathing could sometimes be a difficult task. Though, technically, the summer had turned to autumn only two days prior, it still *felt* like it was summer. The atmosphere was blistering hot and thick with suffocating humidity.

So, William was drenched in sweat. It poured from his brow in an endless flow, soaking the cloth band that lined the inside of his hand-made straw hat. Fast-flowing rivulets of the salty fluid trickled down onto his face. The sweat burned his eyes. He tried to wipe the irritating substance away with the sleeve of his white linen shirt, but it was useless. His shirt sleeve, like every other piece of cloth covering his body, was dripping wet with perspiration. William sighed, frustrated, as he yanked another ear of corn from its dry, dusty, brown stalk. He angrily tossed the corn into his half-filled gathering basket.

"Autumn cannot arrive soon enough for me!" the boy grumbled wistfully. He allowed his thoughts to wander to a cooler time and place. He dreamt of the coming season with its colorful leaves on the trees and cold frost on the tall grass. Oh, how glorious it will be!

Truth be told, William had already grown a bit too accustomed to autumn-like weather. Throughout the first three weeks of September, the people of the South Carolina backcountry had experienced an odd cool spell. On the last day of August, soaking rains and high winds settled upon the region forcing most people to seek shelter inside their homes. The atmosphere became significantly cooler, windier, and wetter than usual. It almost seemed as if the autumn had, indeed, arrived early.

Like most of their neighbors, when the cold rains came,

the Newmans took refuge indoors. William greatly enjoyed the unexpected vacation from most of his normal, everyday farm chores. Other than the daily feeding and tending of livestock, he relished the days of quiet, indoor activities with his loving mother, Lizzy Newman. Indeed, he enjoyed having his mother all to himself for three whole weeks. It was a rare treat, indeed.

William's father, Will Newman, and his older brother, Austin, had been gone throughout the entire cold, rainy spell. They had been serving with the British Loyalist militia somewhere far to the west in South Carolina's Ninety-Six District. The Newman men, along with most of the neighboring farmers, had taken up their muskets and gone to the remote district in service to the King. They went there to defend a frontier fort against a rebel army from the coastal city of Charlestown.

William did not really understand why his father and brother had gone to Ninety-Six, or why Charlestown would send an army against the backcountry villages. He knew nothing of Colonial American politics. He only knew that, throughout the region around Jackson's Creek, the approaching army from the coast had stirred up a frenzy of patriotism and allegiance to King George III. There was much talk of war and a growing revolution.

It greatly disturbed the young lad to hear his parents speaking about the possibility of a shooting war in South Carolina. William did not really understand the concept of war or why men would ever consider fighting a war. Indeed, he could not even imagine the notion of men actually shooting guns at one another. Though there were occasional rumors of raids by the neighboring Cherokee, all that William had ever known or experienced in his eleven years was a quiet, tranquil backcountry life. Indeed, the Newman family had lived in peace in their home on the banks of Jackson's Creek since long before William was born.

Of course, the entire time that her husband and older son were gone to Ninety-Six, Lizzy Newman fretted and worried without ceasing. She was convinced that her men would be "soaked to the bone and starving to death" out in the cold wilderness. But, little William knew better. His father and brother were both experienced outdoorsmen and knew very well how to take care of themselves. And William was right. The Newman men managed to remain dry and relatively well-fed throughout their brief military deployment.

With the coming of the strangely cool weather, William had hoped beyond all hope that the summer season was finished and that they actually were experiencing an early autumn. But, alas, it was not to be. The rain and cool temperatures departed almost as quickly as they had appeared. After three weeks, when the rains stopped, the frontier climate returned to normal for late September in South Carolina. And normal meant unbearably hot and humid.

Three days after the cool spell ended, Will and Austin Newman returned home from their service in the militia. Thankfully, there had been no fighting. The two armies had parted peacefully. Lizzy was thrilled that they were home safe and unharmed. William was equally glad to see his father and brother, of course. But, he also knew that their return from military service meant that his delightful indoor holiday with his mother was over. It was time to get back to the hard work of running a large frontier farm.

It took a few days for the family's corn crop to dry out from weeks of soaking rains. But, finally, the spindly corn-stalks had become completely brown, dry, and brittle. The grain was ready for picking. The Newman brothers were tasked with bringing in the corn and getting it safely stored in the family's corncrib before another round of rainfall arrived. It was their yearly responsibility. As usual, picking the corn would be no easy or brief task. Will Newman's cornfield was huge.

Ten acres of corn, beans, melons, and squashes sprawled across the bottomlands adjacent to the lazy, meandering waters of Jackson's Creek. The field looked like most others on neighboring South Carolina farms. It was actually a "three sisters" food plot that utilized the ingenious methods of the family's Cherokee neighbors.

The "three sisters" was the name that the Indians assigned to the foods that helped them survive each winter: corn, beans, and squashes. All three of those crops could be stored long-term and consumed throughout the cold winter months. When combined with fresh meat, either from farm-raised livestock or wild game, they comprised a nutritious, balanced, and satisfying diet.

Twenty widely-spaced rows of tall corn filled the center of the Newmans' long, narrow field. Along the outside edges of the corn, they planted various types of beans. The bean vines climbed the outer rows of cornstalks and elevated their tasty fruits high off of the ground, making for easy picking. Throughout the field, surrounding the dry, crackling cornstalks, there were hundreds of squash, pumpkin, and melon plants. The large leaves of the ground-covering plants and vines, in addition to protecting the tasty fruit that lay hidden beneath, helped shade the fertile soil and prevent unwanted weeds from growing and choking out the beans and corn. It was a perfect system of agricultural harmony that had been used by the North American natives for thousands of years.

Will Newman's farm plot was a well-designed field, and it had produced an ample crop during the summer of 1775. The bounty of food in this field would serve the family well throughout the coming winter. Indeed, there was probably enough corn on the stalks to trade in Camden Town for other much-needed foodstuffs and supplies. But first, the sun-ripened and dried grain had to be picked, prepared, and stored.

For young William Newman, picking corn was his least favorite job in the entire world. He thought it a great injustice that the task always seemed to fall upon the hottest days of the entire year. He could not, for the life of him, understand why corn did not ripen for harvest in the cooler months of November or December. But, such notions were nothing more than silly dreams in the mind of a farm boy. It was September. The corn was dry and ready. It had to be picked.

As William leaned forward to grasp yet another ear of grain, he suddenly felt a bit dizzy. He gasped for a breath. He knew instantly that he was in danger of being overwhelmed by the heat. The boy needed some relief from the intense sun. He needed it quickly.

Unfortunately, there was no shade to be found in a field full of skinny, dried cornstalks. The leaves had been removed almost a month prior, while they were still green, to save as winter food for the Newmans' cows, goats, and horses. The relentless, blazing sun blanketed the open, bare field with its merciless rays. There was no way to escape its burning wrath.

In the absence of shade, William's body craved water. He searched frantically for his canteen. A large gourd, half-full of water, dangled from a nearby cornstalk. He quickly snatched the gourd from its perch and then knelt down between the rows of naked, leafless stalks. He pulled the cork from the hole in the top of the gourd and took a long, deep drink. The water was not cool at all. Indeed, it was unpleasantly warm. Still, it was wet and at least somewhat refreshing. Seeking more relief from the water, William quickly removed his hat and poured a generous splash on top of his head. He allowed the tepid water to trickle over his neck and then run down the center of his back.

Though the water offered a tiny bit of relief, William felt a little uneasy in his stomach and feared that he might vomit. He closed his eyes and concentrated upon taking a few deep breaths. Unimaginably, for the briefest of moments, William actually dozed. His mind descended into a shallow sleep. Then, quite suddenly and unexpectedly, a deep, familiar voice snatched him from his slumber.

"Boy, are you praying? I declare ... you are not going to get much corn picked down there on your knees."

William's eyes fluttered open and his head whipped around in surprise. Immediately, he realized that his big brother, Austin, was standing over him. The handsome, sweat-soaked twenty-two-year-old rested his hands on his hips. He was grinning from ear to ear. However, Austin's smile evaporated quickly when he saw the distressed look on his little brother's face.

"What is wrong with you, lad? You are as pale as a ghost!"

William frowned. "I do not feel well, Austin. I think I actually fell asleep. I fear that I may pass out from this heat."

"Well, we cannot allow that to happen, can we?" He reached down and grabbed his little brother by the arm. "Come, William. Let us take a little break down at the creek."

"But ... but ... Papa wants this corn picked and in the

crib," William protested half-heartedly as he struggled to his feet. "I would not want him to return home from his trip to Camden and find the job unfinished."

"Do not worry, William. We live in South Carolina. Papa knows how hot it is. Besides, he did not say that we have to get all of the corn in *today*. There is not a hint of rain, and we are not likely to see any for a few days. It will not place our corn crop or winter supplies in jeopardy if we take an hour or so to rest and cool off."

"Are you sure?" asked William, his voice almost trembling with emotion and hope.

Austin smiled reassuringly and then patted his younger brother affectionately on the shoulder. "Yes, I am sure. Come along. Cool water awaits us. Let us get out of these stinky clothes and enjoy some time in our favorite swimming hole."

The two brothers turned and then trudged slowly southward toward the tree-lined creek.

WILLIAM LAY on his back and floated lazily in the shallow waters of Jackson's Creek. His ears were actually below the top of the water. The cold water blocked out all sound. The tall oak and chestnut trees that lined the creekbanks shrouded the water in dark, cool shade. It was so well-shaded that William almost felt as if he were inside a cave. It was pure bliss. He wished that he could float in the luxurious, shaded, cold creek water until suppertime.

A distant-sounding, garbled voice interrupted his solitude and thoughts. William sat up quickly and turned to his brother. "What? Did you say something?"

"I asked if you feel better now," responded Austin, smiling playfully.

"Much better, thank you," William answered with a grateful smile.

The lad balanced himself and sat upon a large rock in the bottom of the slow-moving creek. He faced his brother. Austin was also sitting cross-legged on the creek bottom. The water was chest-deep.

Austin stared at William with a look of brotherly concern. "I was quite worried about you, William. I had to carry you the last twenty yards or so. You did not even have the strength to undress yourself."

William chuckled lightly. "I was a bit concerned, as well. This horrid heat almost did me in. But, now I feel revived by these cool waters." He gently glided his arms and hands along the top of the water, allowing the cool liquid to wash over them. "Jackson's Creek has always provided us a beautiful, refreshing place to rest and swim. We should have done this sooner in the afternoon."

"We have never before been too busy with farm work to take a swim break, have we?" Austin reminded him.

"No, I suppose not."

"Well, we shall not make the same mistake tomorrow. So long as it remains this hot, I say we take swim breaks both in the morning *and* in the afternoon. Agreed?"

William nodded and grinned. "Agreed."

After their brief discussion, they enjoyed a lengthy period of silence. The brothers had long ago decided that words were not always necessary when they were together. They simply enjoyed one another's company. William adored such quiet moments with his older brother.

Though neither of them spoke, Jackson's Creek buzzed

with the many sounds of life and activity. William closed his eyes and listened. There was the unmistakable rattle of a pileated woodpecker as it pounded tirelessly against the trunk of a faraway tree. From a nearby pasture, there came the high-pitched bleating of a calf calling for its mother. Somewhere in the distance, William heard the piercing screech of a red-tailed hawk. The trees overhead cracked and rattled as armies of squirrels jumped from limb to limb, raining acorns and debris onto the waters below. Truly, Jackson's Creek was an unspoiled, magical place for a boy to grow up. William was most grateful for his happy home on the Carolina frontier.

Once again, Austin's voice broke through the silence of the moment. "It certainly is good to be back home." He chuckled. "Though I could do without this horrid heat."

William stared thoughtfully at his brother. He was glad that Austin had mentioned his recent absence from home. He had many unanswered questions about the events in the colony that had compelled his father and brother to join the King's army.

"Austin, why did you and Papa have to go away? I still do not understand why the militia was called up."

Austin shrugged. "We went because the rebels sent an army out of Charlestown to take over the King's fort at Ninety-Six."

"What are 'rebels?'" William inquired curiously. He had heard that word spoken many times recently, but remained unsure of its meaning.

"Rebels are men who take up arms against the lawful government. They are folks whose minds are fixed upon rebellion against the authorities."

"You mean against the governor of the colony?"

Austin nodded. "Yes, and against King George. These rebels recently held an illegal congress and then forced our governor, Lord William Campbell, out of office. Even now, Campbell must take refuge on a Royal Navy ship at the mouth of Charlestown harbor."

"But, why are these rebels going against the King and our Royal governor? I do not understand."

Austin shook his head slightly. "Most folk say it is because of money and high taxes. I reckon the rich plantation owners along the coast have always resented paying their higher taxes. But, when you own a lot of land, taxes to the King must be paid. It is the British way."

"So, then, this conflict is just about money?" William asked, quite alarmed and still somewhat confused. "It is about gold and silver?"

Austin shrugged and nodded. "Pretty much, I suppose."

Now, William was even more confused than ever. "But, often times I have heard our own Papa complain about paying the King's taxes. Recently, I have heard him fussing about the new taxes on paper and tea."

Austin sighed. "If one looks at human history, I rather think that money has always been at the root of most of our wars. So, if there is to be another war here in the British Colonies, I am sure that money and taxes will be pretty high on the list of causes." He paused. "Still, there are some men who do not need much of a reason. Sometimes, men simply want to fight." He shook his head in disappointment. "There is so much evil in our world."

William pondered his brother's words. Still, his curiosity was not satisfied. "But, why would these rebels come way out here on the frontier? Charlestown is a very long way from Ninety-Six. It makes no sense to me."

Austin inhaled deeply. Clearly, he had not intended to be drawn into such a deep, philosophical discussion with his little brother. He considered his words carefully.

"Well, the rebels know that most of the men who live out here in the backcountry districts have no interest in turning our backs on England. We are content with our government and loyal to King George III. So, they sent out their army to make a show of force. They wanted to prove to us that they are sincere enough in their rebellion to make war." He paused. "In the end, though, I really think they were actually hoping to start a fight."

"But, you and Papa did not have to fight while you were away, did you?"

"No. Thankfully, we did not. Nary a shot was fired."

"But, if you did not go to fight, then why did you have to be there at all?" William inquired further. He seemed even more confused.

Austin pondered. "How can I help you understand?" He thought for a moment and then quickly formulated an explanation. "You know how sometimes, when you and I play a game of chess, we must move our pawns or other pieces so that they can protect the King and Queen? Not every move in chess is a winning move. Some are defensive moves."

William nodded. "Yes, of course."

"I suppose you could consider our time at Ninety-Six as something like a defensive move in a very large game of chess. The rebels, obviously, made a very bold move when they came out of Charlestown. They wanted to cut us off from the King. They took a gamble and attempted to take over the entire backcountry by occupying our fort at Ninety-Six. But, we in the Loyalist militia moved swiftly into a position to protect the fort and to show our allegiance to England and to King George." He smiled. "Does that make sense? Does that help you understand?"

William considered his brother's words. He nodded

thoughtfully. "That does, indeed, make sense. It is quite amazing, really. Even way out here in the backcountry, we can still defend our King." Almost immediately, his face morphed into a disapproving smirk. "But, I still do not understand why anyone would be interested in taking over the town at Ninety-Six. I went there once with Papa to sell some horses. It is a most unimpressive little village. There are far too many pigs out there. I would much rather go to Camden Town."

Austin laughed out loud. "On *that* we can agree, little brother. But, still, we could not allow the rebels to have their way. We had to send them a message. They had to understand that their army and their rebellion were not welcome out here on the frontier."

"But, do you think they got the message?" William asked.

Austin nodded confidently. "I believe they did. Almost a thousand Loyalists showed up to resist them. Now, they know for certain that we men of Jackson's Creek and the other outlying districts are very loyal to the British Crown. We stand opposed to their rebel congress. We serve only King George."

William stared thoughtfully at a ripple atop the waters of the slowly-moving creek. He mumbled instinctively, "God save the King."

"Yes, indeed. God save the King," echoed his older brother.

2

CHURCH INTERRUPTED

Six Weeks Later
Sunday, November 12, 1775

S ince its humble beginning in 1771, the Jackson's Creek Presbyterian Church had served as the main gathering place for the residents of the frontier region. It was the heart of the Jackson's Creek community. Besides regular worship gatherings, the church also hosted newspaper readings, political rallies, and various speakers and guests from faraway cities and towns.

Despite its importance as a community center, Sunday morning worship gatherings at the Jackson's Creek Church were ordinarily quite small. However, as talk of war and revolution increased in the colonies, attendance at the weekly church services had been increasing. The Jackson's Creek folk were always hungry for news from outside their isolated, frontier world. Unfortunately, almost every Sunday, there seemed to be more bad news than good.

There was constant talk of the war in the northern Colonies. In Massachusetts, back in the spring, militiamen fought skirmishes against the British Army at the towns of Lexington and Concord. Then, in June, there had been a huge battle near Boston at a place called Bunker Hill. Though several months had passed, people throughout America still talked about these disturbing battles.

Tensions were high throughout the thirteen colonies. The war was steadily creeping southward. Indeed, the recent conflict with the rebels from Charlestown had proven that revolution against England was also coming to South Carolina. The people of Jackson's Creek sensed that their days of peace and quiet were coming to an end.

The Sunday church service was about to begin. The room was packed full of people. As the congregation waited, most folk sat and whispered quietly. Since the church had no "official" pastor, the elders of the congregation took turns each week leading the singing and preaching the sermons. John Phillips, a local businessman and one of the most influential leaders of the church, would preach this week. He sat on a tiny bench beside a handmade wooden pulpit. He was busy making last-minute preparations, reviewing his notes, and thumbing through his ancient Bible.

The children of the Austin and Newman families, next-door neighbors on Jackson's Creek, filled a bench near the back of the church. Their parents occupied the row immediately behind them. Rachel Austin and Lizzy Newman sat next to one another. Bartholomew "Bat" Austin and Will Newman sat on either side of their wives. The adults sat in patient silence as they waited for church to begin.

Will Newman and Bat Austin were the best of friends. They had been so for almost thirty years. They met one another as young men during a chance encounter in the remote South Carolina wilderness. Bat actually saved Will's life on that fateful day, rescuing him from the bite of a venomous snake. Then, over several days, Bat cared for Will and nursed him back to good health. Quite naturally, they formed a deep bond of friendship during that time together.

After that life-changing event, though they lived many miles apart, they wrote countless letters and made occasional journeys to visit one another. Finally, after ten years of long-distance friendship, they settled near one another as frontier neighbors at Jackson's Creek. Such was the depth of their friendship that Will Newman had named his firstborn son, Austin, in honor of his best friend Bartholomew Austin.

So, for almost twenty years, Will and Bat lived next to one another as neighbors and friends. They raised their families together. They dined at one another's tables. They shared all of life's burdens and joys. They were, indeed, the very best of friends. But, in truth, they were much more than that. Though they shared no relationship of blood, they considered themselves to be brothers. They were family.

Lizzy Newman and Bat's wife, Rachel, were also best friends. Likewise, their children were very close to one another. Bat and Rachel Austin had three sons: Drury, Joseph, and John. All three boys were similar in age to Austin Newman, so the young men were quite inseparable. The four rowdy, adventuresome lads had grown up together playing, farming, hunting, fishing, and exploring the forests of the beautiful Carolina frontier.

Bat and Rachel had one daughter. Her name was Mary. She was their youngest child. Mary was eleven, exactly the same age as little William Newman. As the youngest children of the two neighboring families, Mary and William were, quite naturally, playmates and best friends.

Of course, the older brothers thought it quite odd that a boy and girl could be such good friends. Over the years, William and Mary had endured much good-natured teasing from their teen-aged brothers because of their unusually close relationship. The older boys constantly made kissy-faces and poked fun at the younger boy and girl. Indeed, they often proclaimed that William and Mary would someday be married.

Mary and William tried to ignore the endless teasing inflicted by their older brothers. Truly, they did not understand all of the fuss. "*After all*," they thought, "*why can't a boy and girl be good friends?*" To them, it seemed the most natural thing in the world.

Though the grown-ups sat in respectful silence, the children of the two families talked amongst themselves as they waited for the church service to begin. The older boys whispered quietly and respectfully. They took great care not to disturb the people around them. They knew that their parents would never tolerate any unruly behavior inside the church building. Over the years, they had learned very well how to behave while at church. However, it seemed that the younger children still had a few more lessons to learn.

William Newman was, as usual, seated next to little Mary Austin. As was their custom, they were chatting gaily and giggling. They had not seen one another for a few days, and were quite excited to spend some time together. They each had much news to share and many stories to tell. As youngsters will sometimes do, they became lost in the joy of one another's company. Their conversation steadily increased in excitement and volume. William's high-pitched laugh soon reached an unacceptable level for church. The adults around him were beginning to stare at him with disapproving looks.

Bat Austin suddenly leaned forward and gave the loud, unruly lad a resounding thump on the back of his right ear. The boy yelped in pain and instantly covered the wounded, throbbing ear with his hand. It stung so badly that he thought he might cry. However, he could never allow Mary to see his tears. He composed himself, took a deep breath, and then faced forward. He did not utter a single word. Instead, he prayed silently that the aching in his ear might cease.

Mary's eyes were wide with disbelief. She glanced back at her father, covering her mouth with her hand. He lifted his forefinger menacingly to his lips, displaying the universal command for silence. She obeyed, of course. Like William, Mary turned around and faced forward. Neither of them spoke another word. They had learned a most important lesson. They would have to save their conversations and stories for the coming noon-time meal.

Will Newman had observed the ear-thumping incident from his seat at the end of the aisle. He chuckled at his son's crimson face, pained expression, and sudden silence. He leaned forward slightly to make eye contact with Bat. He smiled and winked and then silently mouthed the words, "*Good shot.*" Bat grinned and gave Will a subtle "thumbs-up" in response.

Finally, it was time for church to begin. Mr. Phillips stood and approached the pulpit. He reverently placed his large Bible on the wooden stand and then cleared his throat. The people instantly ceased their whispering. Everyone stared expectantly at the Elder Phillips, eager to hear his Bible reading and words of wisdom.

"Good morning, friends," he declared in his thick native Irish accent. "As we gather once again on the Lord's Day, we must acknowledge that a cloud of darkness and evil hovers over our beautiful land. I know that we are all disturbed by the increasing rumors of war here in the King's colonies of America."

Heads bobbed up and down in agreement. Two of the more vocal men in the church responded with a loud, "Amen!" Little William frowned. He glanced at Mary. She, too, was frowning. Neither of them liked to hear the grown-ups talk about war. But, lately, it seemed that was all they ever talked about.

Mr. Phillips paused and inhaled a deep, thoughtful breath. "We now live in a time of rebellion here in the colony of South Carolina. Men in the cities and towns along our coast boast of waging war against King George. Indeed, it seems that many of them desire to fight a war here ... upon our very own soil." He held his ancient Bible high in the air. "Of course, this comes as no surprise to those of us who know the words of this sacred book."

He paused and stared sternly at the dozens of silent folk who filled the chairs and benches of the church. The people were mesmerized. It seemed as if they were scarcely breathing.

"Folks, I declare that this unholy rebellion against the lawful authorities stands against the Bible and against the desires of our Lord God." Mr. Phillips shook his head in disgust. "Truly, a war here in South Carolina would be a terrible thing. It would be an evil thing. It would cause neighbors to take up arms against one another. Battles would take place in our forests, in our fields, and on our farms. It would be a horrible, bloody conflict, indeed."

The men and women of the congregation groaned in despair. Some of the men actually growled in disgust. They stomped their feet and pounded their fists against the wooden benches. Clearly, the men of Jackson's Creek did not like such talk of war and rebellion. They were fiercely loyal to King George and to England.

William sat quietly on the his bench and listened. His

heart pounded excitedly in his chest. He, too, was moved by the elder's words. They reminded him of the long talk that he and his brother, Austin, had enjoyed several weeks prior. His mind wandered back to the conversation that day when they were resting in the cool waters of Jackson's Creek. Though William still did not understand everything that was going on, it nevertheless angered him that men would rise up against England. It ached him to think of the men of South Carolina fighting against one another.

Suddenly, William felt something warm touching his hand. He glanced downward. Mary's soft, pale hand lay on top of his. The girl was trembling. Clearly, she was very afraid. William scooted closer to her. He opened his hand. Their fingers locked together.

William leaned in close and whispered into her ear, "Do not be frightened, Mary. Everything will be all right. I promise."

The confident sound of his words seemed to calm her a bit. She nodded slightly and continued to stare at Elder Phillips. She did not release her grip on William's hand. The boy smiled. He quite liked holding Mary's hand.

Mr. Phillips lifted his hand to calm the murmuring crowd. "This is the declaration of the apostle named Peter. I read for you from I Peter 2:13-17:

> *[13] Submit yourselves to every ordinance of man for the Lord's sake: whether it be to the king, as supreme; [14] Or unto governors, as unto them that are sent by him for the punishment of evildoers, and for the praise of them that do well. [15] For so is the will of God, that with well doing ye may put to silence the ignorance of foolish men: [16] As free, and not using your liberty for a cloak of maliciousness, but as the servants of God. [17] Honor all men. Love the brotherhood. Fear God. Honor the king."*

The men of the church erupted in righteous emotion. Some rose to their feet. They shouted and waved their hats in the air. The fires of their patriotic fervor were stoked to a frenzy. William actually feared that some of them might shoot their guns inside the church! Quickly, however, Elder Phillips held up both hands as a signal for the men to calm themselves. After a short while, they quieted themselves and then returned to their seats.

"We must honor these words of the apostle. We must be a people loyal to the Bible, to our God, and to our King. Indeed, this is the only acceptable response that one can give in light of recent events in these colonies. My friends, we must never doubt! We people of Jackson's Creek must remain true to our King and to the legal authorities of Great Britain!"

Though the women remained silent and dignified, the men erupted once again from their benches in thunderous affirmation and applause. Many throughout the room shouted, "Hear, hear!" Again, they stomped their feet, shook their fists, and waved their hats in the air.

Suddenly, in the midst of their patriotic display, one of the front doors of the church burst open. The heavy wooden portal swung inward and slammed against the log wall behind it with a mighty boom. The sound was almost as loud as a gunshot. It startled everyone inside the church. Indeed, some of the men reached instinctively inside their coats for their pistols.

A young, rugged-looking fellow stepped through the opening. His face was covered with scruffy whiskers. His clothing was dirty and unkempt, giving the appearance of having been outdoors for many days. He carried a rusty, beaten Brown Bess musket strapped across his back. The people of the congregation stared in silent surprise at the unexpected, unknown, uninvited visitor.

Mr. Phillips demanded, "What is the meaning of this intrusion, young man? Can you not see that we are in the midst of our Sunday worship?"

The fellow reached up and, as a sign of respect, removed his tricorn cocked hat. "I sincerely beg your pardon, sir. I must make an announcement to your congregation. It is a matter of utmost concern to all of you."

"Is this an official announcement from our legal Colonial government ... from the King's representatives?"

"It is, indeed, sir."

Mr. Phillips smiled warmly. "Then, by all means, you may speak."

The messenger nodded respectfully to the elder. "Thank you, sir." He addressed the crowd. "I come to you today on behalf of Major Joseph Robinson of the King's Loyalist Militia. He has sent me here to summon all men loyal to King George and our glorious country, England. Once again, the militia is being called up. Rebels have attempted to recruit the Cherokee to make war against the settlements here in the backcountry."

A gasp erupted throughout the room, followed by excited murmurs. Mr. Phillips stepped down from the speaker's stand and approached the fellow. His face betrayed a look of total disbelief. "You had better explain yourself, young man. What evidence do you offer to support such a disturbing charge?"

"Sir, I serve in Captain Patrick Cunningham's company. Last night we intercepted a train of wagons headed west into the Cherokee country. We confiscated the goods contained inside those wagons. We discovered one ton of lead and a thousand pounds of gunpowder. The Indian agent in charge of the wagons has sworn before a judge that the munitions were intended for the Cherokee." He paused and allowed the people a moment to digest his announcement. "My friends, the rebels in Charlestown are attempting to bribe the Cherokee to wage war upon our farms and homes here on the frontier."

A wave of dismay and anger swept through the congregation. The people were genuinely disturbed. They murmured loudly amongst themselves. Animated conversations erupted throughout the room.

Elder Phillips held up his hand to silence the crowd. They quickly obeyed his commanding gesture. He inquired, "But, young man, if you have already intercepted the wagons, then the crisis has been avoided, has it not? Why summon the militia at this time?"

"Because the rebels are, once again, out of Charlestown. They are headed our way. Their commander is Andrew Williamson, a well-known rebel. He is leading an army to take back the powder and lead. They intend to deliver it to the Cherokee, as planned. Obviously, we cannot allow Williamson's army to succeed. Our very lives and the safety of our farms and families depend upon it. That is why Major Robinson has issued the call for all men loyal to England to join him in the defense of their country."

A quiet, frightened, almost reverent hush fell upon the room.

The young messenger continued, "We muster tomorrow at Nineteen-Mile Creek. I humbly ask all you men to join us there before noon."

"Where will we go once the army is mustered?" inquired Bat Austin.

The fellow shrugged. "We do not yet know the true

direction of the rebel army. We have sent spies to track them. We should know something in a day or two."

"How long will we be gone?" inquired another man, somewhat exasperated. "I cannot abandon my farm for weeks on end. None of us can. We have preparations to make for the coming winter."

The messenger shook his head. "I am truly sorry. I cannot give you any more precise information, sir. I am merely announcing the call-up of the King's militia. But, I would think it wise to prepare for a week, perhaps longer."

Mr. Phillips interrupted the conversation. "I know that some of you still have questions, but we must allow this gentleman to go. His work is not finished until he visits the other churches in our district." He nodded gratefully to the fellow. "Thank you, young man, for your information and announcement. Consider us informed. Our men will respond to your call. You have done your job well. Please continue on your mission."

The messenger smiled proudly. "It is my honor to serve. Gentlemen, please do not turn your back on your country. Peace on the frontier is at stake. Join us at tomorrow's muster. God save the King!"

"God save the King!" echoed the room full of church folk. Though their words were loud, they seemed a bit less enthusiastic than before. The passion of the elder's sermon, so evident only a few minutes ago, had been replaced by an atmosphere of foreboding and dread.

The messenger returned his hat to his head and then swiftly exited the church. A fellow standing near the door closed it behind him. The room was absolutely silent. The atmosphere was thick with tension, awe, and fear.

Elder Phillips turned and marched slowly and reverently back toward the front of the church. He climbed the steps that led onto the platform and then stood behind the pulpit.

"Ladies and gentlemen," he began, "it seems that this horrible war is now here amongst us. I know this is not Boston. There is still no open warfare within our beloved South Carolina. Rebels have not yet taken up arms against the King's soldiers. But, our current situation seems desperate, indeed."

Aaron Winslow, a faithful church member, stood and addressed the elder. "I believe we should dismiss today's service immediately, Mr. Phillips. We must all go and make our preparations. If the muster is at noon tomorrow, we have precious little time to ready ourselves."

Mr. Phillips removed his spectacles, frowned, and nodded. "I agree, Mr. Winslow. Because of this disturbing news, I will now declare our meeting closed. I had plans for more readings and some hymns. However, it seems that our Lord had other plans for us today."

He reached down and solemnly closed the cover of his Bible. "Gentlemen, I encourage you to return with haste to your homes and arm yourselves. Gather ammunition, clothing, and food for a week in the field. Spread the word of this call-up as you go. There are many men of our area who have not come to church today. They must be informed of this situation. They will, no doubt, wish to join us tomorrow. Now, please go. You are dismissed."

The people of the congregation rose to their feet. Immediately, the room exploded in emotion and animated conversation. As the people began exiting the building, the Newmans and Austins lingered near the benches where they had been seated. The children turned and stared expectantly at their parents.

Little William asked his father, "Are you going with the militia, Papa? Are you going out to fight against the rebels?"

Will frowned. "Yes, William. I served during the last campaign, and I will serve during this one, as well. If this news is true, then I have no choice. We cannot risk having the Cherokee make war against us. It is time for action. We must protect our homes." He turned to his best friend. "Don't you agree, Bat?"

Bartholomew nodded grimly. "Yes, I agree. My boys and I will answer the King's call."

Rachel and Lizzy said nothing. They leaned toward one another and embraced. Both women had silent tears creeping down their cheeks. Neither of them wanted to see their husbands and sons marching off to war.

"Come, then," declared Will. "We must gather our gear and rations, and quickly so. We have only one day to get ready."

"But, what of our Sunday dinner?" inquired Rachel Austin in a scolding tone. "Surely, we are not going to allow today's fine feast to go to waste. The meal is already cooked and ready for eating."

"Indeed," agreed Lizzy Newman. "Surely, your preparations can wait until after our meal. After all, how long can it take to pack a haversack and knapsack? We are still going to have our customary Sunday dinner together. I must insist."

"I'm hungry!" declared little William. He stole a glance at Mary. He smiled warmly. "And I want to play with Mary this afternoon."

Will grinned happily. "Yes, of course we will eat Sunday dinner. Let us go and feast and spend the afternoon together as family. If I am going to be camping for the next week, I plan to depart with my heart full of joy and my belly full of hot food."

"Amen to that!" exclaimed Bat, rubbing his belly playfully. "I'm so hungry, I could eat a dead buzzard!"

The members of the two families laughed at Bat's declaration. Together, they happily and hungrily headed out the door of the church building.

3

WAR COMES HOME

One Week Later

The men of the Newman and Austin families, along with most of the other men of Jackson's Creek, had been gone for exactly one week. They were far to the west, once again in the vicinity of the village of Ninety-Six. The families knew of their whereabouts because John Austin, age seventeen, had returned home with a stomach ailment just two days after the militia mustered at Nineteen-Mile Creek.

John was violently ill for the first couple of days after he returned home. So, in addition to her regular chores, Rachel Austin's hours were consumed with caring for her son. Thankfully, by week's end, the young man's health had improved dramatically. Though he remained weak and slept most of the time, he no longer suffered from fever or vomiting. Clearly, he was on the mend, but he was still confined to bedrest.

On Saturday afternoon, little William Newman arrived with a letter for Rachel. It was an invitation from Lizzy for

Rachel and Mary to come to the Newman house for their customary Sunday meal. Even though the men were gone, that was no reason for them to abandon their weekly gathering.

Rachel's heart leapt with joy. After five days of being cooped up in the house with a sick son, she was thrilled to receive an invitation to visit with Lizzy and young William. She quickly penned a short note of acceptance and then sent William on his way. Rachel and Mary were both so excited about the coming day of fellowship that they barely slept that night.

Late the next morning, Rachel packed a picnic basket full of fresh food. After preparing a meal for the ailing John and ensuring his needs were attended, the ladies set out on foot for the Newman house. She and Mary arrived shortly after mid-day. Since all the men were gone with the army, Sunday church service at the Jackson's Creek Meeting House had been cancelled. Instead of a customary worship service, the two women and their youngest children enjoyed a brief Bible reading and prayer time. Then, they sat down to a hearty meal.

Though Sunday was customarily a day of rest, the women decided to make good use of the beautiful afternoon weather and do a little work. They labored together to wash the Newman family's bedsheets and linens. They reasoned that the Good Lord would not be too disappointed in them for performing such a practical and much-needed chore.

So, the four of them heated large pots of scalding water and washed the bedsheets, blankets, and pillow covers. Once the washing was done, the women dismissed the children to go inside and play games together. They would take care of hanging the linens and blankets on the clothesline. In truth, the women wanted a little bit of grown-up "alone time." It would give them the opportunity to gossip and catch up on the local news and small talk.

One hour later, William and Mary were seated on the floor in front of the fireplace hearth. The glow of a crackling fire warmed them against the chill of the autumn afternoon. Both children were smiling and happy and enjoying one of their favorite games. Between William and Mary lay a scattered pile of thin, colorful, six-inch-long game sticks. William stared intently at the disorganized, random pile. He was anticipating his next move in their competitive contest, a popular Colonial game known as "*Jack Straws*."

The sticks that they were using in the game were special, indeed. Will Newman had carved the beautiful game pieces when his older son, Austin, was but a small lad. He made them from the leg bones of a deer. The project had occupied an entire winter of quiet evenings in front of his warm fireplace. Indeed, it had taken him almost two months to carve three dozen identical bone sticks.

After the carving was finished, Will dyed the sticks using natural colors from plants and other substances found on his farm. Twelve of the sticks were colored purple using the juice from dried elderberries. Twelve were a soft yellow-green color made from dried dandelion flowers. The final twelve sticks were colored orange-red. Will used the rust from the surface of an ancient iron rod to make this uniquely colored dye.

Once all of the bone sticks were brightly colored, Will sealed the surfaces by rubbing them with a thick coating of bees wax. A couple of times each year, Will rubbed fresh wax on the game sticks to protect them and to preserve their vivid colors. The game pieces, though they had been made fifteen years ago, still looked as if they were brand-new.

Austin Newman, ten years older than his brother,

William, had played with the sticks throughout his childhood. He often enjoyed games played with his best friend, Drury Austin. Later, though, when Austin was older and no longer interested in children's games, he gifted the set of handmade game sticks to little William. Truly, the lovely gaming pieces were a family heirloom. Over the years, both Newman boys had enjoyed countless hours of fun playing with them.

"*Jack Straws*" was a common and simple game, but nevertheless required much skill and a steady hand. Players started the game by gathering all of the sticks, also known as straws, in a long bundle. One player stood the bundle of straws upright with one end against the floor and then released the bundle. The straws instantly fell and scattered into a random, disorganized pile. After the scattering, players then took turns picking up a single straw. The goal was to remove straws one at a time without disturbing any of the other game pieces. If a player tugged on a stick and, in doing so, caused another one to move its position, that player automatically lost the game.

Both William and Mary had successfully removed seven straws each. The first moves in each game were always the easiest, since players could retrieve the straws that lay scattered around the edges of the pile. But, as the game progressed and they retrieved each straw, the moves became harder and harder.

This particular game had reached a critical juncture. Mary had just made a very difficult pull and had skillfully removed a straw. Now, it was William's turn. Suddenly, the nervous lad found himself out of options. He had to retrieve a game piece that lay tangled inside the complicated, tightly-packed pile. He carefully chose his target, reached for the end of the stick, and then gave it a gentle, slow pull.

The wax-coated straw came out smoothly. But just as the straw cleared the jumbled pile, another that lay across it shifted ever so slightly. It shuddered just a tiny bit ... almost imperceptibly. William winced in frustration. He hoped for a moment that Mary had not noticed it. But, alas, she had seen the game piece wiggle. The jubilant girl leapt to her feet in victory.

"It moved! I saw it! That other stick moved!" exclaimed Mary gleefully. "Game over, William Newman! I win ... again!"

"Doggone it!" groaned William in mild disappointment. "You always win, Mary."

The boy was smiling from ear to ear. He disliked losing, of course. Every boy did. If he had been playing against his brother, or another lad from across the creek, he might have been frustrated or angry, even. But, he did not mind losing to Mary ... not one little bit. She was his very best friend, and unlike the boys of Jackson's Creek, she seldom gloated or teased after she won a game. She was always a good sport, whether she was winner or loser.

"Do you want to plan another game?" asked William as he gathered up the bone sticks.

Mary shook her head. "Not right now. How about a snack?"

William nodded toward the cupboard. "There is fresh milk in the jug. I fetched it myself this morning." His eyes glistened with pleasure. "And if my nose does not deceive me, I believe that Mother made some shortbread biscuits this morning."

Mary clapped her hands together. "Oh, that sounds delicious. Will Aunt Lizzy mind if we sneak a biscuit?"

William grinned and shook his head. "She made them

for the occasion of your coming. We are welcome to enjoy a few, but we must leave plenty for our mothers."

"Of course," Mary affirmed. She turned toward the cupboard. "I shall pour us some milk if you will fetch the biscuits."

"A good plan, indeed. But first, I must put my straws in their place."

William, holding the colorful bundle of carved bone sticks in his hand, stood and retrieved a small, hinged wooden box from the fireplace mantle. He carefully opened the box, lay the game sticks inside, and then closed the lid. He placed the box on the far left side of the mantle and then turned to join Mary in the preparation of their snack.

Mary was busy pouring fresh, frothy cow's milk into two small glasses when the din of approaching horses reached their ears. They could hear the clamor of the animals' hooves striking the hard road. It sounded like there were several horses, and they were moving quickly. Mary smiled happily and clapped her hands.

"Our men must be home! Papa and Uncle Will are back!"

William shook his head doubtfully. "I do not think they would be coming on the roadway at a gallop, not unless they were being chased by someone."

A look of concern washed over Mary's face. "We must see who is coming!"

Instantly, William and Mary ran to the front door and flung it open. Their mothers were standing on the porch steps and staring at the group of approaching riders. William did a quick count. There were twelve men.

Seconds later, the riders were upon them. They reared their animals to a stop a few feet from the porch. The men were unkempt in appearance and clad in linen hunting frocks and wool coats of various colors. Their hats were streaked and stained from sweat. Their breeches were dirt-stained and torn. They bore the appearance of having been in the field for a long time. William instinctively stepped in front of his mother in a protective gesture. The man at the front of the group, obviously the leader, gave a light chuckle at the boy's action. He tipped his rather grimy cocked hat to the women and children.

"Pleasant afternoon to you all."

Lizzy Newman curtsied. "Good afternoon to you, kind sir." She paused and then added, "God save the King."

Several of the men in the group shook their heads and chuckled sarcastically. A shudder went down Lizzy's spine. Clearly, these men were not loyal to King George or to England.

"We do not represent the faraway criminal known as King George, Madam. Quite the contrary. I am Captain John Anderson of the New Acquisition District Militia. We represent the Committee of Safety and the South Carolina Congress in Charlestown. And who might you be?"

"I am Mrs. Elizabeth Newman, wife of William Newman. This is our home and land, granted to us by the generosity of our King."

The captain smiled cautiously. "It is a lovely home and farm, indeed, Mrs. Newman. You are to be commended on its beauty and upkeep. But, I rather think that you should be thankful to your husband for such a pleasant home. For certain, you owe neither King George nor England any thanks for this fine farm. Surely, old King George does not come and helped you plow in the springtime or harvest corn in the autumn."

The horseback men gathered behind the captain snickered sarcastically.

Lizzy's face reddened in anger. "I would be most careful with such disrespectful talk in this area of South Carolina, sir. Your words are nothing short of treason."

Again, the captain chuckled. He stood high in his stirrups and quickly inspected the farm. "I might be inclined to say the same to you, Mrs. Newman. Nevertheless, I am not here to argue politics with a woman. I have matters that I need to discuss with your husband. Is Mr. Newman hereabouts?"

Lizzy's eyes narrowed. "No, Captain. I am afraid that he is away on business right now."

The captain appeared curious. "Business? What manner of business?"

The hair on the back of Lizzy's neck bristled. "*That* would be none of *your* business Captain. But, you may rest assured that, while he is absent, I speak for him."

The captain nodded thoughtfully. There was a most uncomfortable period of silence. The men all stared admiringly at Mrs. Newman. The captain appeared to be a bit befuddled by the outspoken female. Clearly, he had not planned on having words with such a lovely, headstrong frontier woman.

"What brings you way out here to the Camden District?" Lizzy demanded abruptly, breaking the silence. She added sarcastically, "Why are you not back home tending to your own families and farms? Surely, your women-folk would appreciate the presence of your company."

The captain eyed Lizzy contemptuously. "I serve South Carolina, Mrs. Newman. My company is part of a larger militia force under the command of Colonel Richard Richardson. We are currently encamped about four miles east of here, on the banks of the Wateree River."

Lizzy's outlook brightened somewhat. She smiled at the

mention of Colonel Richardson's name. "I am well-acquainted with Colonel Richardson, sir. He visited here in our home only a few months ago. He was my husband's commander during the Cherokee Campaign of 1759." Lizzy tilted her head toward Rachel, never taking her eyes off of the captain. "This is Mrs. Rachel Austin, my neighbor and friend. Her husband, Bartholomew, served under Colonel Richardson, as well."

The captain tipped his hat to Rachel. "The pleasure is mine, Mrs. Austin. So, they served under the colonel in '59? Goodness, that was a long time ago! Truly, we are grateful for their service in the defense of South Carolina. Still, I am afraid that time in our colony's history has little bearing upon our circumstance and mission today."

"What, exactly, is your mission here today, Captain?" Rachel demanded. It was the first time she had spoken to the captain. Her voice communicated noticeably more force and authority than did Lizzy's.

The captain shifted subtly in his saddle. "The colonel has dispatched us, along with several other companies of the regiment, to gather supplies and provisions for his army." He smiled disarmingly. "As you can well-imagine, an army of over two thousand men can be quite difficult, indeed, to keep fed."

A cold shudder shot down little William's spine. He had a sick feeling in the pit of his stomach. He thought angrily, "*They have come to steal our food!*"

The captain glanced over his shoulder and then snapped his fingers. One of his men immediately handed him a leather-bound book along with a small piece of paper. Five other militiamen dismounted. Three of the dismounted men made a beeline toward the barn.

The captain nodded to the other two men and then

motioned toward the house. "Check inside for men and weapons."

Two of the militiamen climbed the steps, brushed past the women and children, and then quickly went inside the front door of the house. Moments later, they returned, smiling mischievously. Crumbs covered their coats. They chewed noisily on the sweet biscuits that Lizzy had prepared for the children. A ring of fatty milk coated the top lips of both men.

"We saw no men inside sir," one of the men announced, spitting tiny flecks of cookie as he spoke. "The only weapon we found was an old bird gun."

The captain nodded. "Leave it be. There is no harm or crime in possessing a hunting gun."

"What is the meaning of all this?" Lizzy protested, her voice crackling in a mixture of anger and fear. "What do you think you are doing? You have no right to go snooping about my home and farm!"

The captain sighed. "We must take a portion of your livestock, I am afraid. My men are merely scouting the barn and make a count of your animals. We will not wipe out your stock, I promise."

Lizzy became somewhat frantic. "My animals? Why ... you cannot have any of our livestock! That is our personal property!"

"During times of emergency, the congress in Charlestown has authorized the lawful removal of provisions from the general population. But, you need not worry, Mrs. Newman. You will be reimbursed in full for your losses." He waved the slip of parchment paper that he held in his hand. "I will give you this voucher, which your husband may present to the magistrate in Camden at the conclusion of our campaign. The district authorities will pay him in currency or coin for the animals."

"And what kind of campaign might you be pressing here amongst the honest folk of the backcountry?" Rachel inquired in a hateful, obviously disgusted voice.

The captain's semi-friendly smile vanished. "Madam, it is a campaign to rid the land of all Tories and Loyalists. We are tasked with arresting all such criminals and bandits and then taking them to Charlestown to stand trial."

"Stand trial for what?" demanded Lizzy in complete disbelief.

The captain appeared amused. "Why ... for rebellion against the lawful authorities of South Carolina, of course."

Little William's eyes burned with righteous anger. He could remain silent no longer. He stepped off of the porch and approached the captain. Standing near the fellow's left boot, he declared boldly, "There is no lawful authority in South Carolina but King George!"

The militiamen laughed at the upstart boy. The captain sighed and then lowered his eyes in disappointment. He paused, then shook his head in a gesture of arrogant disbelief. He glanced at his men. "Now, you see, fellows ... that is *exactly* the sort of treasonous talk that we are attempting to purge from this beautiful land." He winked at the sergeant. "What do you think, Sergeant, should we string this one up? Perhaps a stretched neck will teach these backcountry folk a lesson."

William's heart leapt into his throat. Did the captain *actually* say what he just said? Was he about to be hanged by these thieving rebels?

The sergeant winked back at the captain. "Hanging this little runt would be a waste of good rope, if you ask me.

Anyhow, we have too much work to accomplish today. We have at least ten more farms to visit."

"Agreed," the captain declared, nodding. Then, without warning, he lifted his foot and delivered a vicious kick to William's face. The heel of the man's boot impacted across the bridge of the boy's nose. His nose made a dull cracking sound. William fell backward onto the ground. Blood flowed freely from his wounded face. The crimson fluid stained the front of his tan weskit and white linen shirt.

Lizzy emitted a startled scream. She dropped down to her knees to assist her son. "William, my boy, are you all right?"

William slowly rose to his feet. He pinched his nose shut to stem the flow of blood. "I am fine, Mother. You need not worry about me."

Lizzy stood and stepped between the officer and her son. She defiantly placed her hands on her hips. She shrieked, "You, sir, are a wicked beast! You are certainly no gentleman." Her chin lowered as she glowered angrily at the man. "How brave you must feel ... coming here today to steal from and make your war against defenseless women and children."

There was a small commotion near the barn as the three soldiers exited the building. One was leading a cow by a short rope, one was leading a large hog in similar fashion, and the last man was carrying three upside-down chickens in each hand. The captain observed the men and then quickly jotted a few words on his paper. As the soldiers secured the tethers of the larger animals to their horses, the captain leaned over the neck of his horse and extended the slip of paper toward Lizzy. She made no move to receive it.

"I suggest you accept this document, and thankfully so, Mrs. Newman. You will see that I have noted your contribution of one beef cow, one hog, and a half-dozen hens, and that I have been most generous in my estimation of the weights of the hog and cow. You will be reimbursed well, I assure you."

Lizzy hesitated for a moment and then reluctantly stepped down from the porch. She leaned toward the captain and carefully took the paper in her hand. As she turned to walk away, the captain held tight to the voucher. He gave the paper a slight tug, halting her movement. She lifted her eyes and glared hatefully at the man.

Captain Anderson gazed intently at the defiant, outspoken woman. His face erupted into a taunting smile. "I suggest you control that lad of yours, Mrs. Newman. Next time, I will not be so gentle with him."

He suddenly released the voucher. In disgust, Lizzy jerked her hand away from the man. He politely tipped his filthy cocked hat. "I bid you ladies a fine day." He turned his attention to William. "And I hope you have learned a lesson today, boy."

Both women, along with William, declared spontaneously and simultaneously, "God save the King!"

The captain paused for a moment, smiled, and then shook his head in disbelief. He actually seemed amused at their bold rebellion against his authority. He and the other men turned their horses and then headed back toward the highway. They moved more slowly as they departed, hampered by the creeping pace of the reluctant cow and the short-legged hog. It was several minutes before they disappeared from view. The men appeared to be headed in the direction of the Austin home.

Once they were out of sight, Lizzy slowly sat down on the steps. Her legs were wobbly. Her hands were trembling. Clearly, she was quite shaken by the encounter.

Rachel turned to the children. "William, are you quite all right?"

"Yes, Mrs. Austin. The bleeding has already stopped. Though, I doubt my shirt will ever be clean again."

She waved her hand dismissively. "Do not worry about that. Now, you must run quickly! Go to our house and warn John! Tell him to flee before these men arrive. Tell him to pack for travel! He must go and warn our Loyalist forces of this new army that has come to terrorize our homes."

William nodded. "Yes, ma'am."

"Waste no time! Do not dawdle, boy! John's life depends upon it. If he resists when they try to take our food, they might kill him. Do you understand?"

"Yes, ma'am," William declared once again.

"Should I go as well, Mother?" asked Mary excitedly.

"Yes, Mary. Go with William. You can help John pack his things. And William, while they are packing, I want you to open the barn and release all our cows and goats into the north field. They will likely take refuge in the woods and should be well-hidden from these thieving men."

William nodded his understanding. "Yes, ma'am. I will."

The two youngsters immediately turned, ran to the far end of the porch, and then leapt down onto the soft grass below. Swiftly, they ran cross-country in the direction of the Austin farm.

4

WE MUST SURRENDER

William and Mary successfully delivered their message to John Austin. Minutes before the thieving rebels arrived, John disappeared on horseback into the dense forest to the west. He had only one thought on his mind. He must inform his father and the other men of Jackson's Creek of what was occurring back home. Their farms and their families were in jeopardy.

Two days later, John successfully reached Ninety-Six and located the Loyalist army. He delivered the shocking news of Colonel Richardson's large army encamped in the Camden District. The Loyalist militia commanders immediately called for a meeting with the enemy commanders entrenched against them. They quickly negotiated a truce that would allow everyone on both sides to "declare victory" and depart the field. By the end of the week, the Austin and Newman men were back home.

Even though the men had returned, times remained very grim for the folk of Jackson's Creek. Colonel Richardson's army was still encamped in the district. Soldiers were searching for the Loyalist militiamen who had served at

Ninety-Six. Somehow, they had obtained a list of names of all of the local soldiers. They were arresting the men on that list and sending them back to Charlestown for trial. Sadly, several of the men of Jackson's Creek had already been arrested and taken away in chains. Many others had fled the region, most of them headed toward Florida, where they planned to organize their resistance to the rebels.

Of course, the Newman and Austin men assumed that they were all on the list. It seemed only a matter of time before the rebels came to take them away, as well. Still, none of them wanted to flee to Florida and join the army there. So, they remained at home. As they awaited the arrival of rebel soldiers at their farms, the Newmans and Austins had some decisions to make. Would they remain at home, or might they take refuge in the mountains to the west? Would they resist, or would they submit to the congress at Charlestown? Would they surrender, or would they take up their muskets once again and fight?

Sunday, December 3, 1775
Bartholomew Austin's Home – Jackson's Creek, South Carolina

THE MEN HAD BEEN HOME for over two weeks. It was Sunday … the day of the weekly Austin and Newman family meal. This week it was a supper gathering. The Austins were hosting the meal at their house. After an afternoon of fellowship, music, and games, the two families sat down to dine at sunset.

The ample table was filled to overflowing with two haunches of roasted venison coated with salt and cracked peppercorns. There were four plates stacked high with boiled red potatoes. In addition, there were two wooden bowls filled with thick porridge made from ground corn and wheat flavored with elderberries, blackberries, and hickory nuts. Four plump loaves of fresh, steaming-hot bread filled a single platter in the very center of the table. Dessert was roasted and mashed pumpkin flavored with butter, molasses, pecans, and ground cinnamon and nutmeg. The aromas that filled the house were simply mouthwatering.

The members of both families gathered around the table and then joined hands for a prayer of blessing. Bat, as the master of his home, worded the prayer. Immediately after the prayer-ending, "Amen," Bat declared proudly and emphatically, "God save the King!"

Everyone gathered around the table echoed, "God save the King!"

Immediately, the throng of hungry folk took their seats. They reached for the various bowls, plates, and platters that were scattered across the large oak table. They attacked the tantalizing meal with gusto.

"This venison is delicious, my dear," Bat declared, licking his lips after partaking of a generous bite of the juicy meat. "It is so tender, mild, and moist."

"You have our Joseph to thank for that," Rachel responded. "It is from the young doe that he shot in the north woods last week."

Bat grinned. "I reckon, then, that the both of you are to be commended for this wonderful roast. It is a succulent treat, indeed."

"Enough of the talking!" urged Lizzy Newman, sounding slightly irritated. "All of you hush up and eat."

Everyone gathered at the table laughed happily as they stuffed their mouths full of scrumptious, hearty food.

～

IT WAS about an hour past dusk. The kitchen table was freshly cleaned from the supper meal. Lizzy and Rachel sat at the table sewing, talking quietly, and enjoying one another's company. Little William and Mary played a rowdy game of dominoes on the floor near to their mothers. The four young men: Austin, Drury, Joseph, and John were in the adjacent parlor partaking in a friendly game of cards.

As was their custom, Bat and Will sat contentedly beside the stone fireplace. Bat occupied his favorite rocking chair. Will perched comfortably on top of a short three-legged stool. Both men lazily puffed on their clay pipes and enjoyed a cup of steaming tea as they pondered the world around them and discussed the politics of the day.

"Have you heard anything new about Colonel Richardson and his army?" inquired Will. He lifted his pewter mug to his mouth and then took a satisfying sip of his fragrant, honey-sweetened tea.

Bat made a circle with his mouth and lazily blew a series of perfect smoke rings. "Not much. I heard a little talk in town yesterday. Rumor has it he is currently encamped somewhere across the river from Camden."

Will frowned. "That is too close for comfort, if you ask me."

"What about you?" inquired Bat. "Have you picked up on anything new?"

Will inhaled a deep, thoughtful breath. "I have been hearing about many more arrests this past week. People say Camden has already been emptied of all men deeply loyal to the King. Most others have simply surrendered themselves to the rebel army."

Bat nodded grimly. "They have that list of names. I am sure that Colonel Richardson is being most thorough as he seeks out all of our compatriots in arms."

Will declared, "To be honest, I am surprised that we have not yet received a visit."

"It is only a matter of time, I am sure," Bat prophesied. He grinned playfully. "Perhaps the good colonel is just saving the best for last."

Austin smiled. He was about to respond when, suddenly, somewhere in the distance, a chorus of hounds unleashed a frantic din of angry barking and mournful howls.

"I wonder what has disturbed your dogs," Will mused.

Drury Austin called anxiously from the parlor. "Papa! There are men out front!"

"Who are they?" demanded Bat nervously. He sat upright in his chair.

"I am not certain. They do not look familiar to me," answered Drury.

"How many are there?" inquired Will.

"I count eight, all on horseback."

Little William jumped to his feet and ran to the nearest window. He declared excitedly, "They must be soldiers! They're those mangy rebels, I'll bet!"

Rachel rose from the table and approached Bat nervously. "It must be Richardson's men." Tears crept down her cheeks. "Oh, my heavens! They have come for you, Bat! Surely, they will take you all away from me!"

Bat smiled lovingly at his wife. He cupped her tender cheek with his hand. "Calm yourself, my dear ... let us not jump to any conclusions."

"Two men have dismounted!" little William shrieked excitedly. "They are coming up the steps!"

Seconds later, there came a loud rapping on the front door. Bat scanned the expressions of his friends and family members. Clearly, they were all concerned. The women were obviously very frightened.

"I will answer the door," Bat announced. "It is my house, after all. The rest of you should be about your business. Try not to arouse any suspicion."

A muffled voice called from beyond the door, "Bartholomew Austin! Are you home? I must speak to Mr. Bartholomew Austin!" Again, a fist pounded loudly against the door.

Bat walked to the door, lifted the latch, and opened it. He stared at the two men who were standing on his front porch. They wore muskets on their backs and had pistols tucked inside their leather belts.

"I am Bartholomew Austin," he announced. "How might I be of service to you at such an unholy hour of the evening?"

The older fellow of the two reached up and tipped his hat politely at Bat. He spoke with a pleasant Scottish accent. "I am truly sorry for the late hour of our arrival, Mr. Austin. I am pleased to make your acquaintance. I am Captain Lewis McKenzie of the Craven County Militia. This is Lieutenant Angus Clinkscale. Might we come inside for a moment and have a word with you?"

"What is this regarding, Captain McKenzie?"

The captain hesitated slightly. "I am here as a representative of Colonel Richard Richardson, commander of the forces of South Carolina."

Bat's heart skipped a beat. They were, indeed, rebels from the east. He stammered, "Yes, of course. Please pardon my ill manners. Do come inside."

"Thank you, Mr. Austin." He paused. "But, before we do... would you kindly allow me and my men to take refuge in your barn for the night? It is quite frigid outside. Darkness has fallen, and we are all a bit chilled. We need a warm place to stay. Some shelter from the cold would be most appreciated."

"Of course, Captain. Your men will find ample hay and water for their horses in the barn. But, for their personal shelter, I would invite you to use the small cabin near my east pasture. It has a fireplace and is well-stocked with wood. We keep it prepared for travelers and guests. It is quite cozy, indeed, and should serve you well."

"Excellent. I am most grateful for your generosity, sir." He turned to his aide. "Lieutenant, will you please see to the men and then return here once they are settled into the cabin?"

"Are you certain, Captain?" The younger fellow cut a suspicious glance at Bat. "I should not wish to leave you here alone."

"Get to it, Angus. These are good people. They pose no threat to me."

"Yes, sir." The young officer nodded and then departed quickly.

"Please, come on inside, Captain," Bat invited. "Are you hungry? Would you like some tea?"

The captain smiled warmly. "I am quite famished, indeed. And a spot of tea would be delightful."

"Come along, then. My wife will be happy to fetch you some, as well as some supper."

The captain removed his cocked hat and cloak as he entered the home. Little Mary Austin stepped forward and politely received his garments. She hung them on a peg board near the door. The captain stepped into the warm front room. The members of both families stared at him and remained completely silent. Little William did not attempt to hide his emotion. He glared at the man with a detesting, angry look.

The captain smiled, somewhat amused by the little boy's obvious defiance. He inquired, "What is happening here? Is it some manner of a party?"

Bat chuckled nervously. "No, Captain. 'Tis no party. It is merely our weekly Sunday gathering." He pointed to his family. "This is my wife, Rachel, and our children: Drury, John, Joseph, and Mary. The other folk are the Newmans, our life-long friends and nearest neighbors. We ordinarily take a meal together on Sunday."

"Newman, you say?" He turned to Will. "Would you, perhaps, be Mr. William Newman?"

Will stepped forward and shook the captain's hand. "Yes, Captain. I am Will Newman." He pointed to his family members. "This is my wife, Lizzy, and our sons, Austin and little William."

The captain smiled warmly. He extended his hand to Will and they shook. "It is truly a pleasure to meet you all."

Bat grabbed two ladderback chairs from the dining table. "Come and join us by the fire, Captain. We have nothing but porridge and bread left over from our supper. I am sorry that I have little else to offer you."

"A bowl of porridge and a slice of bread would be a blessing indeed, Mr. Austin. I have not had hot food in almost three days."

"Come, then. Sit down and warm yourself by the fire while the ladies fetch your food," invited Bat. He gave a subtle nod to his wife. She and Lizzy immediately began to prepare the officer some supper.

The three men sat together near the hearth. Bat sat, once again, in his rocking chair and Will returned to his stool. The militia captain sat in one of the ladderback chairs. Everyone else sat at the table or hovered within earshot, anxious to glean whatever information they could from the surprisingly friendly rebel. The men enjoyed small talk for a while as Rachel and Lizzy ladled porridge from the warming pot and carved thick slices of bread.

Minutes later, the young lieutenant returned from his errand to join them. Seating himself in the other chair, he reported that the soldiers had fed and sheltered their mounts and were in the process of occupying the cabin. The ladies then served both of their guests a generous portion of leftover porridge, a large wedge of bread, and a pewter mug full of steaming tea.

The two soldiers nodded gratefully. The captain declared, "Thank you, ladies. You are most gracious and kind, indeed."

The two ravenously hungry men devoured their hot, filling supper in a matter of minutes. Afterwards, they continued to thaw their hands and feet near the toasty fire as they relished in the luxury of a cup of fresh, fragrant tea. Bat shared a generous portion of his pipe tobacco with each man. Soon, the four gentlemen were all sipping tea and smoking their clay pipes. It almost appeared as if all of them were old comrades who had gathered for some Sunday talk and a friendly smoke. However, the circumstances and politics of the day remained heavy upon all of their minds.

After a few minutes of shallow chatting and small talk, Will could stand the suspense no longer. He needed to know the purpose of their visit. He demanded bluntly, "What brings you here tonight, Captain? Obviously, this is not a social call. You did not come all this way to drink tea with us."

The captain inhaled a deep, thoughtful breath. "Unfortunately not. I assume, of course, that you are aware of the presence of our army and our mission here in the backcountry."

Will glanced briefly at Bat. He then turned his attention quickly back to the captain. He nodded. "Yes, Captain. Rumor says that you are rounding up all Loyalists, especially those who took up arms against Williamson at Ninety-Six."

"Yes. That is true." Captain McKenzie affirmed. "And I believe that both of you were there."

"We were, indeed," Bat responded unashamedly.

"And your sons were with you?" confirmed the lieutenant.

Will inhaled deeply. Reluctantly, he responded, "Yes."

The captain smiled thinly. Some of the friendliness vanished from the face. "I have been dispatched here on a personal errand by Colonel Richard Richardson. I believe that both of you know him well."

"We do," Will affirmed. "Mr. Richardson and I were once neighbors, when I was a lad. He and my deceased father were very close friends. As a matter of fact, Bat and I both served in his regiment during the Cherokee uprising in '59."

The captain nodded thoughtfully and drew deeply on his pipe. "The colonel has informed me of this, as well. That is why he dispatched me here today to invite you and your sons to travel to our encampment headquarters. He wishes to speak to all of you personally, as friends and former comrades."

"All of us?" Will asked, confused.

Captain McKenzie retrieved a slip of paper from his weskit pocket. "These are my instructions." He scanned the paper. "I have been ordered to escort Bartholomew Austin and his sons, Drury and Joseph Austin, along with William Newman and son, Austin Newman, to Colonel Richardson at his headquarters in Camden Town." He folded the paper.

"The colonel wishes to speak to the five of you immediately."

"And if we refuse?" asked Bat pointedly.

Captain McKenzie turned toward Bat and looked deeply and honestly into his eyes. "Please understand, Mr. Austin. Colonel Richardson harbors no ill will toward any of you. He merely wants to have a personal conference with you. He wishes to obtain your surrender and then grant you an official pardon. He has already had the papers prepared and approved. They only await his signature." He paused. "But, if you decline his kind invitation, we are ordered to compel you to accompany us to Camden."

"I see," responded Bat glumly. "You will arrest us, then."

The captain nodded. "Yes. If necessary. So, you see, it would in your best interest to come with us willingly. The colonel has spoken fondly of you both. I believe that he has your best interests at heart. From our brief conversations, I know that he wishes to issue your pardons with haste and then send you back home to enjoy lives of industry and prosperity."

Bat looked at Will. Will smiled and nodded to his friend.

"It is a generous offer, Bat," Will mumbled softly. "We cannot deny that."

Bat nodded in agreement. Both men stood. Immediately, Captain McKenzie and Lieutenant Clinkscale stood, as well. Bat sighed in defeat as he offered his hand to the captain.

"Very well, then, Captain McKenzie. We offer you our surrender. We will voluntarily accompany you gentlemen to Camden tomorrow. Should we leave our guns at home, or must we turn them over to you?"

"No, Mr. Austin. None of that will be necessary. I rather think that you fellows will need your weapons for your return trip. One never knows what dangers he might encounter out here in the backcountry." He smiled, much more warmly this time. "We shall depart at first light, so that you gentlemen will have plenty of time to return home before nightfall."

"Thank you, Captain," Bat responded gratefully. "We are most grateful for your honesty and your attitude."

Rachel and Lizzy appeared in the midst of the men. Rachel carried the iron pot from the fireplace crane. Gripping a thick wool potholder around wire handle, she handed it to the lieutenant. Lizzy gave the captain a large basket covered with a linen cloth.

Rachel explained, "Please take the remainder of this porridge and bread to your men, Captain McKenzie. There are also a few boiled potatoes in the basket, along with a small box of salt. I am certain that your soldiers will sleep better with their bellies full of hot food."

The captain bowed slightly at the waist. "Thank you, Mrs. Austin. My men will be very happy, indeed. They are weary of hard bread." He nodded to Bat and Will. "Until tomorrow."

"We will meet you at the barn at dawn," promised Bat.

The Whig militiamen moved swiftly toward the door and made a quick exit. Bat slowly closed the door behind them as they departed.

Little William turned to his father. His face was filled with a look of disbelief. "Papa, what does it all mean? Are we no longer servants of King George? Are we going to join the rebels?"

Will patted the lad on the shoulder. "No, William. We are not joining the rebels. It just means that neither Bat nor I, nor any of our sons, will fight again. The enemies of our King now control our district. They are in charge. So, while they are in charge, we must obey them. If we do not, we risk going to jail."

"Or worse," added Bat.

"Worse?" asked young William nervously. "What could be worse than jail?"

"They could hang us," Will responded ominously.

"Oh, my!" little William groaned. "That would be ghastly! Well, then ... we have no choice. We must surrender!"

"We?" Will Newman chuckled proudly at his son. He glanced at the faces of every member of the two families gathered in the room. Despite the circumstance, everyone was smiling. "Yes, William. We have no other choice. Our war is over. We must surrender."

PART II

SHIFTING ALLEGIANCES

5

THE BRITISH ARE COMING!

Five Years Later
February 16, 1780

"I do wish that you would allow Austin to help you," declared Lizzy Newman. "You know that he would not mind doing so."

"We have already had this discussion, Mother," William responded flatly. "Molly is *my* horse. Caring for her is *my* job. And I am quite capable of handling things on my own. Besides, Austin has his own interests, if you must know."

Lizzy cocked her head and eyed her son suspiciously. "Whatever do you mean?"

William grinned shrewdly and shrugged. "I hear tell he has his eye on a young lass down Winnsboro way. According to one of my friends, she is some wealthy shopkeeper's daughter. He has probably gone there to court her this very night."

"Nonsense!" retorted Lizzy, waving a dismissive hand in front of her face. "You know as well as I that your brother does not care the least about romance or marriage. All the boy cares about is spending every waking hour with his mischievous friends. Lord only knows what trouble he, Drury, and John are stirring up this evening."

"Perhaps," agreed William skeptically. "Still, I would not expect him to return until well after your bedtime."

Lizzy sighed, ever-concerned. "Likely so. And I shall not sleep a wink until I hear the door latched shut behind him upon his return."

"You will likely lay awake half the night, then," teased young William.

His mother grunted proudly. "Here ... take this food with you," she ordered, quickly changing the subject. She placed a cloth-covered basket on the table beside her son. "I foresee that you will get hungry during the night. Goodness knows you have a most healthy appetite."

William grinned gratefully. "Thank you, Mother. These will be welcome, indeed."

"And button that coat tightly!" she barked. "'Tis a frigid night. I fear that it may even snow before the sunrise. I can smell it in the air."

Lizzy stepped closer to wrap a heavy wool scarf around her son's neck. Because of his height, she had to reach upward in order to accomplish this ordinarily simple task. As she tied the heavy cloth, she shook her head in proud disbelief. She could scarcely believe that her baby boy, now sixteen years of age, was approaching six feet in height.

In truth, William Newman actually towered over his mother. He was every bit of a foot taller than she. He was a handsome, muscular, broad-shouldered young fellow. His thick, sandy brown hair was medium length and pulled back from his face into a short queue. He sported a two-day growth of thin, irregular whiskers on his prominent, angular chin. Little William Newman was no longer "little."

He had grown into a fine, upstanding, hard-working young man.

Lizzy finished tying a snug knot in the scarf and then reached up to touch her son's face. She lovingly stroked his cheek and then, as mothers often do, reached upward to tuck a stray twig of loose hair back into its proper place.

"I know that I shall worry over you all the long night," she declared in a soft voice that was filled with loving concern. "It is sure to be dreadfully cold outside, and you have neither fire nor hearth to warm you."

"I doubt that I shall freeze to death in my own barn," responded the handsome, brown-haired young man. "I have slept there countless times." His eyes twinkled with mischief. "Besides, I have all those horses and goats to keep me warm."

"Humph!" grunted his mother with displeasure. "Such a notion does not relieve my worry over you one bit. Sincerely, son ... please be wise and take care of yourself. I will pray for you without ceasing."

William smiled gratefully. "I covet those prayers, Mother."

Suddenly and without warning, the lad leaned forward and planted a sloppy, affectionate kiss on his mother's cheek. She shrieked with delight. As his mother hovered near him, he grabbed her shoulders, lowered his chin, and then vigorously rubbed his spiny whiskers against the soft skin of her neck. It was one of his favorite tricks to play on his mother. He knew how she absolutely *hated* the feel of itchy whiskers. He had seen his father perform the same trick on her hundreds of times. He was so very proud that, at his relatively young age, he had sufficient whiskers to imitate him.

"Will Newman!" Lizzy screeched at her husband,

pushing futilely against her son's chest. "This boy of yours is in desperate need of a shave! If he goes one more day without cutting those horrid barbs from his face, he could lose his status as a gentleman."

Will Newman, resting in his favorite chair beside the fireplace, had been sitting quietly and watching the playful interaction between his wife and son. He suddenly erupted in joyous laughter and winked at William. His teeth gleamed orange-gold in the glow that emanated from the fireplace. He sat upright, placed his smoldering pipe on his smoking table, and then rested his arms comfortably across his chest. He stared admiringly at his son.

"I doubt that the livestock will care if he is sporting a beard tonight. Worry not, my love. Little William shall not fall into ill repute on this farm! The moment that he decides to ride with me into Camden Town and show his face publicly, I will hold him down and shave him myself. I promise." He added, with a playful wink, "But, William ... surely little Mary Austin will never want to kiss you whilst your face is covered with those itchy whiskers."

Little William's face flushed a deep crimson. He released his mother from his playful embrace, turned quickly, and then retrieved the basket full of food from the table. "I must go now," he proclaimed, suddenly uncomfortable and impatient. Clearly, he had no desire to speak of his youthful romance with the lovely Mary Austin. He stammered, "I ... I ...do not want Molly to be alone when her time comes."

His father nodded, still smiling. "Go on, then, boy. Give us a loud shout if there is a problem or if you need anything. I will be more than happy to help."

"I will, Father," William promised as he turned toward the door. "But I think that I will be just fine. 'Tis not my first time to help with a foaling. 'Twill not be the last." He bent over and retrieved several other items that lay in a ready pile beside the door.

"I love you, Son," his mother announced proudly. "I will have you a hot breakfast prepared and ready at sunrise tomorrow."

"I love you, too, Mother." He smiled. "Make it a big breakfast, for I know that I shall be famished."

"Every breakfast in this house is a big one, as well you know it," Lizzy retorted proudly. She playfully shoved him toward the door. "Off with you, then. And do try to get some sleep!"

William shrugged. "I hope that I can, but I doubt there will be much opportunity for sleep tonight. This is Molly's first foal. It could take many hours."

Grabbing a candle lantern from its nearby hook, he lifted the latch on the door and then disappeared quickly through the opening. He nimbly hooked the toe of his leather shoe on the bottom of the door and skillfully used his foot to pull it closed behind him. The door banged against the doorjamb. Almost instantly, the latch dropped into its cradle with a familiar wooden pop.

A cold wind nipped at William's cheeks as he stepped down off of the porch and into the yard beyond. It was a cold, dark, spooky winter night. The piercing wind whipped at the tall oak trees beyond the barn. Their limbs, reaching high into the gray-black moonlit sky, had been stripped clean of their leaves during the autumn. The skinny fingers of bare wood swayed to and fro in the wind, emitting an odd chorus of clicking sounds as the dry limbs impacted and rubbed against one another. The air was wet, indeed. Lizzy Newman was correct. Rain or wet snow would likely fall before the dawn.

William shivered at the thought of snowfall. He did not

care for winter precipitation. He pulled his collar tightly beneath his cheeks, thankful for the scarf that his mother had placed around his neck. He was also thankful for the delicious supper that he had just enjoyed. It felt good to have a belly full of warm, comforting food. He would need the hearty fuel to keep his mind alert and his body warm and functioning throughout the coming night.

William breathed a sigh of dread. It could prove to be a long, stressful night, indeed. He was worried. Molly was his beloved horse. He had known her throughout her entire life. He had been present for her birth and had raised her for his own. The two were inseparable. Normally, he rode her daily. But in recent days, the discomfort of the foal growing inside her had relegated her to a quiet life in the barn and corral. At the tender age of five years, she was still a young mare. This was her first birthing. William could not help but be concerned for her well-being, especially after the traumatic events of the previous winter.

One year prior, William had watched helplessly as two of his father's best mares died while foaling. Sadly, only one of the foals survived. Because of those traumatic memories, the handsome young fellow could not dismiss the possibility of disaster from his mind. He was petrified at the very thought of losing his beloved Molly.

It almost seemed that the elder Will Newman could read his son's mind. For the past several days he had been reassuring William that young Molly was a fine, healthy horse and that she would have no problem delivering her foal. Still, William could not help but fret over the animal, for she was more than just his horse. She was his friend and constant companion. And because of their intimate relationship, he simply could not allow her to endure the task of giving birth alone in a dark, cold barn. He would remain with her until it was accomplished. Nothing could keep him from it.

William trudged determinedly toward the barn. As he walked, he gathered his thoughts and began to prepare his heart and mind for the coming task. He tried to reassure himself that foaling was a natural process and that everything would turn out fine. Though many hours of pain and distress lay ahead, the end reward would be new life. By the coming of the dawn, there *would be* a new member of the Newman clan's barnyard family.

"*Tomorrow will be a day of celebration!*" he promised himself.

William smiled at the thought. He could not wait to look into the huge, black eyes of Molly's newborn foal. The thought of it compelled him to pick up his step, despite the heavy load of cargo that weighed upon him.

Besides the lantern and basket filled with tasty smoked meat, fresh bread, and dried fruit, William carried several other necessities that would help keep him warm and occupied throughout the night. His left coat pocket contained eight thick, new beeswax candles ... more than enough to keep all of his candle lanterns lit until sunrise. He carried in his right coat pocket a copy of *Robinson Crusoe*, his favorite novel. Beneath his right arm he cradled a plump, heavy goose-feather pillow. Finally, on his back he bore three large, heavy wool blankets rolled into a tight bedroll and secured with a leather strap.

Earlier in the afternoon, he had prepared himself a thick nest of fresh, clean straw in a corner of Molly's stall. The thick, luxurious blankets would work in concert with the thick straw of the makeshift bed to keep him warm and comfortable ... when and if he actually had the opportunity to sleep.

William, motivated by the bite of the cold wind, trotted the last few steps to the barn. Finally reaching the large door, he lifted the latch and immediately stepped inside. He placed his cargo on the ground beside the door and then quickly pulled it shut behind him. He felt immediate relief from the cold wind. He could see very little inside the barn. Even with his one-candle lantern, it was dreadfully dark.

"Goodness be! It is as dark as a cave in here!" he proclaimed cheerfully to all the occupants of the barn. "How is everyone in the barnyard tonight? Are you all as excited as I?"

Several horses snorted in response, happy to hear his familiar voice in the darkness. Agnes, his father's old plow-horse, grunted and stomped an excited foot on the hard-packed earth in her stall. It was her familiar way of demanding sweet, tasty oats.

"No oats for you at this late hour, Agnes," chastised William. "Breakfast time is still afar off." The old horse emitted a long, disappointed groan, almost as if she understood the lad's words.

William walked to a nearby table upon which sat two candle lanterns identical to the one that he carried. He opened the front of the burning lantern and removed the candle. Quickly, he used its dancing flame to light two more candles. He then placed them inside the other two lanterns. Almost immediately, the warm, yellow glow of the three mirrored lanterns illuminated the interior of the barn. Curious horses, along with a handful of skinny goats, stared at him over the gates and from between the boards that enclosed their cozy stalls.

"There!" William proclaimed to no one in particular. "That's better. Now, I must check on my girl."

He walked swiftly to a nearby stall and opened the gate. He gazed lovingly at his faithful horse.

"I am here, Molly. How are you doing, my dear?"

The chocolate-brown Marsh Tacky mare was lying on her side. Slowly, and with some effort, she lifted her head and looked at him. She exhaled a weak snort. Her eyes twinkled in the candlelight. She seemed comforted by his presence. Almost immediately, though, she lay her head back down on a crushed pillow of hay. Her huge, swollen belly heaved. The muscles of her sides and back seemed to quiver. Her breathing was shallow and somewhat irregular. The birthing mama was obviously in pain. One way or another, her baby was coming, and soon.

William frowned. He hated to see his sweet Molly in such distress. He desperately wanted a foal from this lovely animal. But now, as he watched her panting and grunting in pain, he greatly regretted his decision to breed her.

"There, there, girl ... it will not be long, now," he declared in a calm, soothing voice. He was unsure if he was speaking to calm the horse or to calm himself. He leaned forward and rubbed her soft nose. "I will be right here with you until the little one comes."

Molly's ears flicked in response. It was not her normal, happy way of communicating with William. But, on this particular night, it would have to do.

He knelt beside the animal and patted her gently on her neck. After a moment of thoughtful pause, he rose and then stepped out of the stall to retrieve his blankets and pillow. Returning quickly, he unfolded and spread the blankets and prepared a comfortable cocoon in his soft bed of hay. He also retrieved the other two lanterns and then hung them on nails driven into posts on opposite sides of the stall. Once everything was prepared, he nestled beneath his soft blankets and then took out his book.

"If you do not mind, Molly, I will read a bit whilst you do your work. You may summon me when you need me."

Molly slowly lifted her head and peered wide-eyed at him. He smiled at her. Seemingly reassured, she lay her head down once again and then proceeded with the labor of birth.

William was half-way through the first chapter of his book when he heard the distant clip-clop of a horse's hooves upon the road. Minutes later, the door of the barn swung open, allowing a breezy wave of frigid air to rush through the barn.

"Close that cursed door!" William barked. "We are trying to keep warm in here!"

Almost immediately, the barn door slammed shut. William listened as his older brother, Austin, guided his own horse to its stall. It took only minutes for Austin to remove her saddle, cover her with a blanket, and then fetch her some grain. Soon, his smiling face, set aglow by the soft light of the candles, appeared over the top of the gate of Molly's stall.

"How is your girl?" he inquired. "Any sign of a foal yet?"

William stuck a stem of hay into his book to mark his spot, closed it, and then lay it aside. "She is as well as can be expected, I think. She was already on the ground when I came out after supper. It should not be long now."

"Do you want me to stay the night with you? I do not mind," Austin offered.

"No, Brother, I will be fine. If I need any help, I will be sure to make plenty of noise." William smiled. "But, I appreciate the offer."

Austin nodded. "As you wish. I am going to go and thaw

my feet by the fire and then bury myself in my bed. I will see you at breakfast."

William nodded politely. "Good night, Austin. Sleep well."

"Good luck, William." He called to the horse, "And good luck to you, Molly."

The anguished mare lifted her tail and then instantly dropped it against the floor with an annoyed thump. Both Austin and William laughed.

THE SOFT, gray glow of a cloudy dawn was barely peeking between the boards of the barn. A thin layer of wet snow covered the ground outside, causing the light of the pre-dawn to seem a bit brighter than usual. The frozen ground of the Newman farm lay silent beneath a cold, white winter blanket.

William awakened with a start. He was quite disoriented. He sat up groggily and rubbed his red, raw, sleep-deprived eyes. He detected the tantalizing smells of smoky bacon and fresh bread. It was morning. His mother was already up and busily preparing the family's breakfast. William's stomach growled. Suddenly, he realized that he had not eaten a single bite of the food that his mother had prepared for him the evening before. But, how could he have possibly taken time to eat? His night had been far too busy. And, oh, what a wonderful night it had been!

The process of the birthing had been breathtaking to him. But, it was the spunky little foal that impressed him the most. Only minutes after he was born, the little fellow had struggled clumsily to his feet. He was wobbly at first, but less than a half-hour later he was scampering and bouncing about throughout the stall. The newborn was naturally curious and most energetic. William fell instantly in love with the little one. His hair was a deep, dark brown ... just like his mother. But, he had one distinct mark. He sported a small, bean-shaped white spot between his eyes. Upon seeing that spot, William knew instantly what he would name the curious little foal. For the rest of his life, this horse would be known as Bean.

It did not take long for the foal to discover the joy and pleasure of nursing his mother. The voracious baby found his mother's breast and quickly filled his empty belly with his first meal. William giggled with joy after the little one finished his breakfast. The foal wandered from his mother, frothy milk dripping from his chin. He ambled over to where William lay and then instantly plopped down onto the bed of hay. William covered the foal with one of his blankets and soon the little one was fast asleep. Seconds later, William joined him in slumber.

But, now, the glow from outside testified that a new day was dawning. William was unsure how long he had slept. He assumed that it had been three or four hours. William reached to his left and touched the warm body of the still-sleeping foal. The little fellow had wiggled close to William and cuddled against him in search of warmth. William smiled. He rolled over onto his elbow and stroked the foal's stiff, pointed ears. He rubbed its perfectly round, muscular jaw. The foal wiggled slightly and emitted a high-pitched moan of contentment.

On the other side of the stall, Molly was on her feet. She munched happily on a pile of oats that William had poured for her into a makeshift trough. The droopy-eyed mare was exhausted but otherwise healthy. Occasionally, she cut a glance toward her baby, her protective motherly instincts on constant alert. But it seemed clear that she was not worried. She trusted her master with the care of her little one.

William, exceedingly happy and relaxed, reclined his head against a mound of hay. He was in no hurry to leave his warm nest. The foal was a very warm and welcome sleeping partner. He was comfortable and content. Indeed, he felt as if he could spend the rest of his days snuggling with the spunky little horse. He reasoned that he might doze a bit more before breakfast. His father or brother would come and fetch him as soon as it was ready.

Suddenly, a sharp noise snatched him from his slumber. It was a gunshot! Moments later, the thunderous throbs of a galloping horse reached his ears. Then there was another gunshot!

"What the devil?" cursed William. He rose, stretching stiffly. Quickly, he sprinted from the stall and, grabbing his coat, headed toward the barn door.

A shrill voice punctuated the silence of the early morning. "Uncle Will! Austin! Come quickly!" It was the familiar call of their neighbor and friend, Drury Austin.

William stepped outside the barn. Simultaneously, his father, brother, and mother came from inside the house onto the large front porch. William trotted across the snow-covered yard to join his family.

"What is all this shouting and gunfire about, Drury Austin?" demanded Will Newman. "You about made me choke on my tea and biscuit!"

Drury leapt from his horse. An excited, joyful grin filled his entire face. Clearly, whatever information he carried, he was most enthused about it.

"Well!" He exclaimed excitedly, "Have you all heard the news?"

Will cocked his head to one side. "What news? Is something wrong?"

Drury's face beamed. "No, Mr. Newman! Everything is very right!" He stared at the Newmans wide-eyed, but said nothing else.

Austin prodded his best friend. "Don't just stand there grinning like a goat eating briars, Drury! Tell us!"

Drury blurted, "The British have arrived!"

Will Newman's back stiffened. A look of joy mixed with concern filled his face. He peppered Drury with questions. "What do you mean? Who? Where? When?"

Drury could not stop grinning. "General Clinton has landed his army on Simmons Island, south of Charlestown. They came from the sea, by golly! Clinton landed his entire army on the beach and then set up camp. Ain't that a fine 'howdy-do!' The Regulars are in South Carolina! Soon they will march against those cursed rebels in Charlestown!"

"Good Lord!" exclaimed Lizzy.

"How many men?" Austin demanded grimly.

Drury shook his head. "I have heard different numbers. But, folks say it is somewhere between 5,000 and 10,000 troops."

Will glanced at his wife and sons. Clearly, the man was stunned by the news. True, they had been surviving under the heavy hand of the independence-minded rebels for five years. Life had been difficult for them, but they had prospered. And since receiving their pardon from the Whig government in 1775, South Carolina had experienced relative peace. The Newman family members stood in contemplative silence as they digested this life-shaking news.

Finally, Austin reflected, "I reckon this changes everything, doesn't it?"

Drury nodded excitedly. "Indeed, it does. The King's

army has arrived! Soon, these rebels will pay a dear price for the many ways they have mistreated us Loyalists. Once old General Clinton gets hold of them, they will regret what they have done to us these past five years. Soon, they will know the fury of King George!"

William had suddenly forgotten the joy of the night and the beautiful, sinless, carefree foal that lay sleeping in the barn. Almost instantly, his mind shifted from the glory of life to the dread of death. Dark images of soldiers and war clouded and overshadowed his happy thoughts. He glanced at his father. "What will we do now, Papa?"

Will rubbed his whiskered chin as he pondered his younger son's question. After a long, thoughtful pause, he answered, "Nothing. We will do nothing right now. British victory is not a certainty. We must wait and see what happens."

"Oh, Will! We have had peace in our district for so many years now," moaned Lizzy softly. "They have been hard years, to be sure. But, at least there has been no fighting nearby to us. No blood has been spilled in Camden or Fairfield Districts. Are those days over now?"

Will nodded. A cloud of concern hovered over him. "Yes, my darling. I fear so. I had hoped that this war of revolution would remain afar off in the north. But, King George's army has arrived. Now, I fear that war will soon be coming to our beautiful backcountry. And it will not just be a war of Continentals and Redcoats. It will be neighbor against neighbor ... friend against friend." He stared forebodingly into the distance. "Soon there will be blood in our beautiful forests and fields."

6

DOUBTS

FIVE MONTHS LATER - JULY 4, 1780

I t was a perfect day, and a pleasantly cool one for the month of July in the Carolina backcountry. Majestic pines swayed lazily in the soft summer breeze. Thick, puffy, white clouds occasionally shrouded a hazy sun. The rapidly moving waters of the Broad River flowed loudly over the rocks of a nearby sandbar. Together, the quiet chorus of summer wind and dancing water seemed almost hypnotic. It was a perfect day, indeed, and a perfect place. William Newman and his present company traveled over ten miles to reach this picturesque picnicking spot.

Still, it was not so much the lovely environment and surroundings that lifted the heart of the dashing Mr. Newman. Rather, it was the young woman who accompanied him to this lush meadow overlooking the majestic Broad River. For, seated on the opposite side of their dining blanket was his very best friend and, without question, the love of his life, Mary Austin.

Mary and William had grown up together. They lived on adjoining farms for as long as each of them could remember. Since there had been no one else approaching their age in the immediate vicinity, they naturally grew to become best friends and companions. They had been playmates throughout their childhood, exploring the fields and forests of the wild country of Jackson's Creek. Truly, they were children of the frontier and the outdoors. They loved their unspoiled backcountry home. Still, even more, they adored one another.

But over the past year, their relationship had experienced an unsettling season of evolution. Mary was quickly developing into a strikingly beautiful young woman. And no one could doubt that William had grown into a strapping, handsome young man. Throughout their childhood years, Mary and William had often talked of growing up, getting married, and having their own farm on the banks of Jackson's Creek. In those early years, such talk had been the fanciful musings of children. But, with their maturity and coming of age, the tone of their discussions changed. Indeed, lately they spoke little of such things. It was far too uncomfortable and embarrassing. The notion of a future together seemed entirely too real, too imminent, and too certain. Idle and childish talk of such grown-up matters no longer seemed appropriate.

As they sat together alongside the river, William suddenly found himself captive to one of those glorious, awkward, uncomfortable moments. He peered longingly at his lovely companion. Mary's youthful beauty almost stole his breath. She was an innocent, lovely fifteen-year-old girl. She had deep, sky-blue eyes and a tiny, pointed nose. Her smooth skin, like the skin of most girls of the backcountry, was tinted with a healthy tan, the sign of a life lived in the sunshine.

Mary sat most ladylike upon her corner of the blanket, several feet opposite from William. Her light green petticoat spread out around her like a giant mushroom. She wore a pale yellow linen short gown and a white linen bonnet. The bonnet was topped with a lovely straw hat decorated with a green silk ribbon that matched her petticoat perfectly. Curly wisps of her shiny black hair dangled from beneath the edges of the bonnet.

William was most thankful that, as he stared at the lovely girl and lost himself in her beauty, she did not interrupt the magic of his moment by looking back at him. Instead, Mary peered silently toward a nearby field, pretending to give interest to some distant farm animal. Despite the pretense, Mary knew full-well that William Newman was examining her. She sensed his gaze. His attentions pleased her. Her lips bent into a subtle, thin smile.

Mary interrupted William's admirations with a sudden and unexpected question. "Have you heard from your brother?" Her head turned slowly and her dazzling eyes met his.

William gulped softly. Though caught off guard by her question and her gaze, he managed to form a coherent answer. He shook his head. "Not since he left for Camden Town to join the Loyalist militia. Once the British Army arrived in South Carolina, Austin could not wait to join the cause." He chuckled lightly. "Mother is worried sick over him, of course."

She nodded knowingly. "My mother is much the same. She frets incessantly over my brothers." She inhaled a deep sigh. "We have heard nary a word from Drury nor John since they left to join the King's militia. Like your brother, they were dying to join in the fight." Her voice trailed away to a woeful whisper. "I pray that they are safe. I hope that I shall see them again. Of course, I always include your brother, Austin, in my prayers."

William was touched. "Thank you, Mary. But, you must believe that they will be fine," he assured her confidently. "There has not been much fighting out here in the back-country. The boys are likely bored stiff with camp life and half-starved, to boot. They will return home soon enough, I imagine." He grinned playfully. "Once they tire of eating camp biscuits and shoe leather, they will wander back in search of some of our mothers' tasty home cooking."

Mary laughed lightly. Then, an unnerving quiet descended once again upon their picnic. Mary appeared lost in thought. She stared toward the waters of the river, but it seemed as if she were actually looking *through* them. In her mind she journeyed to some distant, faraway place. At long last, she broke her pondering silence.

"You realize that today is a very special day for some of our neighbors," she declared matter-of-factly.

"Indeed?" William responded, somewhat confused. "How so?"

"Today is the fourth day of July."

William's face remained blank. Clearly, he was confused. "I do not understand."

Mary cut curious eyes at him. "They call it 'Independence Day,' William. It is the anniversary of the declaration of separation from Great Britain. Four years ago, I think."

William grunted with mild disgust. "Oh, yes ... of course. Back in 1776. But, I do not see why you should trouble your thoughts with the holidays and commemorations of traitors."

Mary turned her head and, once again, looked back toward the river. "William, do you truly understand it all?"

"Understand what, Mary?"

"The rebellion. This war of revolution," she responded quietly. "What are all these men, including our brothers, fighting over, really?" She turned her head and looked to him with a sincere, questioning gaze. Clearly, the girl was troubled in her heart and struggling in her mind.

William shrugged slightly. "Well, *we* are all fighting for King George and Great Britain."

"Why so?" she demanded in quick response.

William cocked his head, confused by her question. "Because he is our Sovereign. We owe him our allegiance."

"But, why?" she retorted immediately. Her voice harshened.

William inhaled a quick, annoyed breath. He was disturbed by her questioning and her tone. "*Because*, Mary, we are British citizens and the King's subjects. It is a deep conviction that our two families share. You know this to be true. We *must* be loyal to our King."

"I see," she mumbled. Her face betrayed a look of skepticism. "My father answered my questions in *exactly* the same manner. Almost word for word. I find it a bit odd, actually."

"Are our responses not sufficient for you?" William's question was quick and sharp. This time, he was the one who manifested a demanding tone.

Mary's head cocked ever-so-slightly to one side. She peered deeply into his eyes. She seemed to be searching his heart. "'Tis not a matter of sufficiency, William. I would simply like to hear some more honest and candid answers to my questions. I dislike receiving the same rote responses from everyone in my family." She paused, then added, "*And* in yours."

William was more than a little dumbfounded and uncomfortable. Mary's questions flirted with the very boundaries of treason against the King. It sounded as if she were challenging not only *his* convictions, but those of her own family members! What could possibly motivate her toward such a line of inquiry? What could cause her to harbor any secret doubts about following and serving the King of England?

"I fail to understand your queries, Mary. Indeed, I must confess that I am somewhat disturbed by them. Do you not hold to the same convictions as the men of your family?"

She lowered her head and, seeking to escape the discomfort of the moment, pretended to busy herself with flattening a wrinkle in her petticoat. "I suppose that I do. I understand them, at least." She paused thoughtfully. "But, William ... I can also understand those who hold to opposing convictions."

"Oh, really?" William responded, a surprised cracking in his voice. "How so?"

"Do you not have friends who are now counted amongst the rebels?" she challenged.

William nodded. "I do. Several, in fact." He smiled warmly. "Isaac Garrison is a particularly good friend of mine. His father is in the rebel army, somewhere far away in the north. He talks often of joining him. I have encouraged him not to do so, of course. I tease him all the time for being a 'lawless rebel.' He, in turn, chastises me for being 'blindly loyal' to King George. But, we laugh it all off and continue to spend and enjoy our time together. Despite our differences, I count Isaac amongst my closest and dearest friends."

"That is a good thing, William. But, have you given thought as to why Isaac and his family think so differently than you and yours?"

"Not particularly," he answered, shrugging. "The foundations of our beliefs have never been a subject of much conversation when we are together. We are simply friends. We have chosen not to let such things come between us. After all, that is what true friends must do."

Her eyes peered stonily into his. "So, then, you are not tempted or afraid to take up arms and fight against Isaac and his father?"

"By no means!" William exclaimed. "God forbid! I shall never fight against any of my friends!"

Mary raised a skeptical eyebrow. "Your response seems a bit unrealistic to me," she retorted coolly. "Indeed, I would say that it is quite naïve."

"Naïve?" he exclaimed indignantly. "You wound me, Mary! Do you truly consider me to be afflicted with shallowness of thought?"

She inhaled deeply. "No, William. I know that you are a candid and thoughtful young man and given to deep and abiding convictions." She paused as she considered her next words. "But, I foresee a day when your convictions will be put to the test."

"How so?" he demanded hotly. His jaw clenched. His face flushed red. His pulse throbbed in his temples. He almost growled, "Please forgive me, Mary. My emotions are a bit raw right now. But, I must insist that you explain this unpleasant prediction."

Her eyes displayed a look of panic. Clearly, William was becoming quite disturbed. It was not the response that she had intended to elicit with her honest questioning.

"Oh, William! Please do not be displeased or upset with me. I care deeply for you. You know this to be true. That is why I *must* ask such things of you. Do you not know and believe that I care for you?"

He nodded ever so slightly. His demeanor calmed a bit. "Of course, Mary. We have been friends and companions for as long as I can remember."

She smiled her familiar, friendly smile. "Good. Please listen, then, to my voice and hear my heart. My dear

William, I fear that circumstances may soon force you to choose from amongst your friends. The British Regulars and George Washington's Continental Army are battling it out in the northern Colonies. True, the British Army is now in Charlestown and beyond. But, this is no ordinary war in South Carolina."

"How so?" inquired William, intrigued.

She sighed thoughtfully. "I foresee that it will not be fought by great armies lining up in front of one another and slaying one another in droves. In our colony it is, in every sense of the word, a civil war. It is neighbor against neighbor. Sometimes, it may even be even brother against brother. It sounds to me that you have already chosen *your* side in the war. But, a day is coming when you may have to choose from amongst your friends, as well."

He shook his head slowly as he digested her words. "I simply cannot agree with you, Mary."

She sighed. "I doubt that my brothers ever thought they would be taking up arms against their neighbors. But, look at them now. Both Drury and John are serving in the King's Loyalist militia. Yet, at this very moment, Andrew and Ellis Carver, their lifelong friends and mates, serve in the rebel militia. They are on opposing sides, William! They now patrol the countryside in the Camden and Fairfield Districts in search of one another. And, one day, they *will* meet. Then, they will be forced to fight face-to-face in battle. Friend against friend." She paused. "Blade against blade."

Such a notion appeared to unnerve William. He shuddered slightly. "Well, I hope that such a horrid day never comes." His voice was tainted with anguished doubt.

"As do I ... with all my heart." Mary reached across the blanket and placed her soft, smooth hand upon his. Her caress was warm and tender. It demonstrated great care and a depth of emotion. "But, the time is coming when *you* may have to make such a choice, William. You are approaching a military age. I daresay, you could probably ride out to an encampment today to volunteer yourself, and some Loyalist colonel would gladly receive you into his regiment. But, will you go? Will you make war against your own neighbors and friends?"

William's chest heaved in a wave of violent anguish. He moaned with great emotion, "I do not know, Mary. I simply do not know! It is a most unbearable thought."

There was another long, painful pause in their conversation. In the midst of the discomfort, Mary withdrew her hand from William's. She turned and, once again, stared beyond the river toward a distant pasture. The silence between them was deafening.

"Please do not be disappointed in me, or offended by me, Mary," William pleaded, almost in desperation. "I cannot abide such conflict or disturbance between us. I care for you far too much."

She shook her head slightly. "William, I am neither disappointed nor offended. I am just worried."

"Worried about our brothers?"

She inhaled a deep, thoughtful breath. She faced him once again and stared deeply into his eyes. She appeared broken and almost on the verge of tears.

"No, William. I worry about you. You *must* know how I feel about you. I worry for our future and our plans together." She paused. Her face displayed anguish and concern. "And I worry that our families may be committed to the wrong side in this ghastly war."

Three Hours Later

WILLIAM AND MARY spoke little during the carriage ride home. Both seemed absorbed in thought. The content of their earlier conversations weighed heavily upon them both. Also, the lateness of the hour was troubling to William. The sun was almost below the western horizon and they still had another three miles yet to travel. Thankfully, William knew the way home well enough to negotiate the roads in the darkness. But, he feared that Bartholomew Austin, Mary's father, would be furious at him for keeping her out after dark.

"We should have started for home sooner," William grumbled, slapping the reins and urging his horse, Molly, to increase her speed. "Your father will have my hide for keeping you out so late. 'Twill be a great scandal, for certain."

Mary nudged him playfully with her shoulder. "You need not concern yourself with my father, William Newman. I have him well under my control. Besides, he knows that I am safe when I am in your care. And I shall make sure that he does not skin you. Not today, at least."

William cut his eyes at her and grinned. After their deep conversation earlier in the afternoon, it felt good to see her return to her more normal, playful self. He clucked at Molly and guided her northeast along the rutted road that led toward Jackson's Creek. Behind them, the sun plunged below the distant hills and painted the western sky in glorious hues of gray, purple, and pink.

"What is that?" asked Mary suddenly. Concern filled her voice. She pointed ahead and to their right.

William fixed his eyes upon a strange vision just above the horizon in the blackening eastern sky. There was an odd, dome-shaped light glowing far beyond the trees. But, it was not just glowing. The dome seemed to shift and dance. A gray vapor hung low over the eerie, yellow-orange, dancing light.

"It is a fire!" exclaimed William. "And a big one!"

"Is the forest on fire?" Mary asked, voice trembling. "Will it block our travel?"

"No." William sounded grim. "It must be a structure ... a barn or house."

"Who lives over that way?"

William thought for a moment. He exhaled grimly. "It could be the Garrison farm."

Mary gasped. "John Garrison? The rebel, and father of your friend, Isaac?"

William nodded grimly. He maintained his gaze upon the distant glow.

"Oh, William!" Mary exclaimed frantically. "Something horrible must have happened! We *must* help them!"

Worry and fear flooded William's soul. He slapped against Molly's rump with a wicked crack of the reins. "Hyah!" he exclaimed. "Go, Molly! Go!"

The mare instantly followed his command. Lurching forward, she seemed eager to run. The ancient, rickety carriage rattled down the bumpy, dusty roadway. William feared that the old rig might shake apart. The orange glow beyond the trees seemed to grow in size and intensity. Suddenly, fingers of flame appeared over the tops of the trees.

"Oh, William! I can see the fire now!" shrieked Mary. "Please go faster!"

"Molly is in a full trot!" shouted William over the loud impacts of the horse's hooves and the grinding of the wooden wheels against the hard-packed road. "She cannot go any faster with this rusty old carriage in tow. It is barely safe for travel at a normal speed. It would not be safe for us, or for her."

"Oh, what tragedy!" wailed Mary. "I hope it is merely a smokehouse or shed."

William shook his head solemnly. "I do not think that to be so, Mary. That is a big fire. I fear it is either the house or the barn."

Several agonizing minutes later, the carriage rounded a curve in the road. Immediately, a blazing inferno came into view. The majestic Garrison home was fully engulfed in roaring flames. The upper floor had already collapsed into a heap atop the first floor. Soon, the entire house would be in ashes. Curiously, the barn and two other outbuildings were burning, as well.

"What in the world?" groaned William as he pulled on Molly's reins. The horse skidded to a stop in the roadway immediately in front of the farm. Though the house was a hundred yards away, the searing heat of the massive fire burned menacingly against William's skin. The horse recoiled and snorted at the unpleasant heat and biting smoke.

"I do not understand," Mary mused aloud. "How can *all* of the buildings be on fire at once? What manner of horrible accident could cause such a thing?"

"This was no accident," William growled angrily. "This was deliberate. Someone has torched this farm!"

Suddenly, William spotted two dark forms on the ground half-way between the house and the road. They were bodies. Both lay face-down on the lawn. His heart instantly fell into the pit of his belly.

"Oh, my Lord!" he exclaimed. "Someone is injured!"

Ignoring the scorching heat of the fire, he leapt from the

carriage and ran full-speed toward the prone bodies. Mary did not move. She remained as still as a statue, frozen in place inside the carriage. She clung so tightly to the side rail that her knuckles turned bleach-white.

As William ran, he could tell from the clothing that one of the victims was male and the other female. He reached the male first. There was a spent musket lying near the body. He knew immediately who it was. He could tell by the familiar sandy-blonde hair. It was his good friend, Isaac Garrison. Dropping to his knees, he quickly rolled the lad over onto his back. He gagged in repulsion when he stared into Isaac's frozen, gray, lifeless eyes. There could be no doubt. Isaac was dead.

William immediately examined Isaac's body to identify the cause of his demise. Curiously, there were no burns upon his body. Instead, a huge pool of blood stained the front of the fellow's weskit and shirt. In the center of his chest William discovered a large hole, obviously from a large caliber musket or pistol ball.

There was nothing that he could do to help his dead friend. So, quickly, William turned his attention to the woman. He gently turned her over onto her back. It was Mrs. Agnes Garrison, Isaac's mother. Her eyes were closed. He leaned forward and placed his ear over her mouth. Feeling the moist warmth of her shallow breath, he experienced a small wave of relief.

He lifted his head and called out to Mary, "Isaac is dead! He has been shot! But Mrs. Garrison is alive!"

William's excited declaration served to jolt Mary from her frozen trance. She jumped from the wagon in a most unladylike manner and then began to run toward William.

"No!" he commanded, pointing at her. "Stay where you are! The fire is too hot!"

She froze mid-run. Obediently, she instantly returned to the safety of the wagon. William stood quickly, bent low, and then grabbed the injured woman beneath her arms. Though she weighed almost as much as he, the adrenaline that coursed in his arteries and veins injected a wave of unusual strength into his members. He swiftly and easily dragged her toward the carriage and safely away from the heat of the fire. He soon reached Mary.

"Is she burned?" shrieked Mary frantically, kneeling beside the stricken woman.

William gave the unconscious Mrs. Garrison a quick examination. He saw no burns. He did, however, discover a rather large knot and a trickle of blood on her right temple. A sizable lump swelled the entire side of her head.

"I see no burns. But, it appears that she has been hit over the head," William explained. "She is out cold, but I believe she will live."

"What is that in her hand?" Mary interjected, pointing.

William glanced down at the woman's hand. Her fist was clenched around something. Prying her rigid fingers open, he removed a crumpled piece of paper.

"How strange ... it looks like a document of some sort." He held it up and examined the writing in the glow of the house fire. "Good Heavens!" he groaned madly.

Mary placed a hand on his forearm. "What, William? What is it?"

"It is a warrant calling for the arrest of John Garrison on the grounds of treason against the King. It is sworn by the magistrate in Camden Town." He continued reading. "It also authorizes the confiscation of his land and property by the Crown."

Mary was aghast. "But, William, I do not understand. Everyone knows that Mr. Garrison is in the Continental

Army and likely stationed in Pennsylvania or Virginia. Who would serve such a document upon his family? And who would make war upon a woman and her children in the absence of her husband? What manner of men would do such a thing?"

William shook his head. His heart pounded like a bass drum inside his chest. His emotions were running out of control. He felt anger, pity, indignation, and rage ... all at the same time. The wave of explosive emotions churned inside of him like a giant, boiling cauldron.

William examined the back of the piece of paper. "This is an official British document," he declared with a broken voice. He held the wax seal upward for her to see. "It was served upon them by Camden District Militia. It bears the King's seal."

She gasped. "So, then ... *our* allies perpetrated this. Men who hold to the politics and alliances of our fathers murdered young Isaac, injured his mother, and burned their home to the ground. Lord help us! It could have been our own brothers!" She emitted a forlorn groan, stood, and then peered helplessly at the raging fire. "But, where are Amy, Sarah, Michal, Finney, and little baby Teddy?" She turned to face William. Her eyes were filled with stinging tears. "Where are the rest of the Garrison children?"

Darkness overwhelmed William's soul. He stammered, "I ... I do not know. But, surely they are not ... " He gulped. "Surely they are not in there!"

William rose to his feet and then stood beside Mary. He draped a protective arm across her shoulders. Supporting one another, they stared helplessly into the indescribable flames. Together, they prayed that the Garrison children were somewhere ... anywhere ... else.

7

BREAKING POINT

The Morning After

The emerging sunrise revealed a thick blanket of fog upon the backcountry. For the sleepless and exhausted William Newman, the ghostly cloud that hugged the ground seemed entirely appropriate. Just as the fog covered the land, so also a shroud of anguish, rage, and guilt covered the hearts and spirits of all the members of the Newman family.

Agnes Garrison had been the lone survivor of the attack upon the farm. She remained unconscious, sleeping on a pallet of soft straw inside the bed of the Newman family's wagon. Lizzy Newman was there with her, bathing and tending to her visible wounds and injuries.

Across the yard, William sat on a small bench beside the Garrison family's stone well. Mary Austin rested silently beside him. William and Mary's soot-stained hands were clasped tightly together. The anguished teens drew all the strength that they could from one another. Nearby, the elder

Will Newman was bathing his hands in a bucket of fresh water.

William and Mary stared in complete horror and disbelief at a large piece of canvas that lay in the center of the lawn. It covered the bodies of Isaac Garrison and all five of his younger brothers and sisters. Tragically, the children had perished in the smoke and flames of the house fire. As he gazed upon the soiled canvas, William's heart was torn asunder.

Mary cut a concerned glance at William. She noticed that a silent tear streaked downward through the soot that covered his right cheek. "Oh, dear William," she moaned softly. "Are you quite all right?"

William sat proudly upright. Feeling somewhat ashamed of his display of emotion, he quickly wiped the tear from his face. "Yes, Mary. I am fine. Do not concern yourself over me."

"But I am concerned for you," she whispered softly. She reached out and cupped his chin with her hand, gently turning his face toward hers. She wanted to see his eyes. She needed to glean his thoughts. "William, you have seen things this night that could break the spirit of a man."

His eyes shifted back toward the canvas that concealed the dead. "At least I am still alive." He sighed. "Already, I am far better off than those poor children."

William looked back to Mary. His tormented gaze was filled with questioning and confusion. "Mary, I do not understand. Where are all the other people from Jackson's Creek? How can it be that my parents were the only ones who answered your call for help? Surely, the flames of this fire were visible for many miles. Where are all our neighbors? Did you not sound the alarm far and wide?"

She nodded. "I did, William. I traveled half-way to

Winnsboro, shouting and screaming as I went. I knocked on the doors of homes, rousting people from their suppers. I called out to any and all who would listen that the Garrison home was in flames. I *begged* for their help." Her chin dropped sullenly. "But, no one would come. Indeed, some responded to my pleas with horrible, hateful, evil words."

William's entire body became rigid with anger. He almost growled, "What manner of evil words?"

Mary seemed afraid to tell him. She shook her head. "I ... I would rather not say."

"Tell me now!" William's command was biting and filled with anger and accusation.

Mary extracted her hand from his and then turned to look away. "William, it was the kind of talk that you might expect from folk loyal to the Crown. Some said that they would not lift a finger to assist a rebel." She gulped apprehensively. "A few others said that the Garrisons probably deserved it."

"Deserved it?" shrieked William, incensed. He jumped to his feet and pointed at the charred remains of the home. "Are you telling me that some of our neighbors and friends believe *this* to be justice? Do they truly believe that these children should have died in their beds ... and all because their father serves in the Continental Army?"

Tears streamed down Mary's face. She wept openly. She had no words. Sharing in William's anger and shame, she buried her face into her hands.

"Where is your father?" William demanded angrily. "He is noticeably absent this morning. Does he share the sentiments of our so-called friends? Does *he* believe the Garrison children received their just reward for their father's politics?"

Mary shook her head timidly. "I did not go to our house

to inform my father. Surely, he does not even know what has happened."

"And why not, Mary? You went to my home, but not to your own? That makes no sense to me. Your house sits only a quarter-mile beyond ours. Why did you not go there?" He inhaled a deep, angry breath, and then hissed, "Were you afraid of what *he* might say ... that he might respond as all of our other neighbors did?"

"Oh, William!" she wailed indignantly. "How could you even *say* such a thing? How could you make such a horrible accusation toward my father?"

"Mary, I demand an answer! Uncle Bat should have come! You should have ..."

Suddenly, Will Newman walked up behind his son and grabbed him by the arm. He spun the distraught lad around so that they faced one another. "That will be quite enough, William! It is over! There is nothing that could have been done for the Garrisons, anyway. The house and buildings were in ashes by the time your mother and I arrived." He paused and glanced at the lumpy canvas. "The little ones were already gone before you even arrived. No one could have survived those flames."

William refused to look at his father. His pulse raged. His face flushed red with fury. Will, still clenching the boy's arm, gave it a strong, muscle-crushing squeeze. The sharp pain snatched William out of his paralyzing rage. He lifted his eyes to meet his father's. As his son calmed, Will slowly released his grip on the boy's arm.

"William, you must control yourself. Please do not take your anger out on our sweet Mary. The poor lass rode for miles last night. It is not she who turned her back on the Garrisons. It was the other folk. It was our neighbors."

"Oh, Papa!" William groaned.

Then, almost as if he were a small child, he tumbled into his father's arms. He buried his face into Will's shoulder. His chest heaved in great convulsions as he wept openly and without shame. Will wrapped a comforting arm around his boy. Quick as a flash, Mary appeared by William's side. She, too, wept. Will reached out with his right arm and pulled her close. The strong father stood, silently, and held both teen-agers as they unleashed a torrent of pent-up anguish and emotion.

After a while, their heart-wrenching cries melted into soft sobs. When the moment had finally passed, William leaned toward Mary and brought his lips near to her ear. He whispered almost imperceptibly, "I am so sorry, Mary. Truly, I am. You know that I love you."

She whispered back, "I know." She did not say anything else. She did not need to. Gently, tenderly, she kissed him on his cheek.

~

The Newman Farm
July 11, 1780

ALMOST A WEEK HAD PASSED since the deadly attack. Thoughts of the Garrison family still consumed William. Agnes Garrison finally regained consciousness. Her body would heal. But, her mind and heart were completely shattered. She had not spoken a word since Lizzy broke the news to her about the deaths of all her children.

The distraught woman's eyes constantly bulged wide, revealing a state of madness. She refused to sleep. She refused to eat. William could scarcely bear to look upon the grief-consumed woman. In his heart, he doubted that she would ever recover, even if her husband were to somehow return home safely from the war.

Meanwhile, the broken woman lay confined to William's comfortable bed. The lad had graciously given up his sleeping quarters to serve as her temporary hospital room. He, in turn, banished himself to the barn. He slept in the loft above the horses. The isolation suited him. After the horrors of that unspeakable night, he had little desire to be around people. Indeed, his anger still burned against his neighbors along Jackson's Creek. He did not feel that he could ever forgive them for turning their backs upon a helpless woman and family in such a time of need.

In order to escape his bitter thoughts, William decided to fix his mind upon other things. There was only one way that he might banish the memories of that dreadful night from his mind. He needed to work. Ever since he was but a small boy, farm labor had always been his best mechanism for clearing his mind and mending his spirit.

The south hayfield needed to be cut and the hay stacked. It was a searing-hot and backbreaking summer task. It was the perfect job for helping a young man to forget his troubles. William filled two gourd canteens full of water from the well. He then fetched a freshly-sharpened scythe from the barn and immediately set out for the distant field.

William lost himself in the work. He attacked the hay, swinging the huge blade from side to side in a violent, sweeping motion. When he first began, with each strike of the blade, he let loose great shouts and groans of pent-up anger. After a while, though, his spirit seemed to calm. He fell into a steady rhythm as he rocked his hips back and forth and guided the scythe skillfully and easily through the juicy shafts of the tall, green grass.

Two hours later, he had cut almost a third of the hay in

the field. He realized that he could not keep up such a rapid pace. Already, his hands ached with blisters, despite the heavy leather gloves that he wore. The muscles of his legs and hips burned and throbbed. And he was parched. There were precious few clouds in the sky, and the July sun bathed the field in relentless heat. It was time for a break. Though he had already drained the water from both of his canteens, his still body ached for hydration. He needed to drink some cold water and take time to rest.

William wandered toward the edge of the field closest to Jackson's Creek. He leaned the handle of his scythe against a pine tree and then slowly trudged toward the edge of the dark, slow-moving water. He knelt on the bank of the creek, removed his wool floppy hat, leaned forward, and then thrust his entire head below the surface of the water. Holding his breath, he paused there and allowed the icy liquid to cool his face and head. Then, when he could hold his breath no longer, he sat up. He allowed the refreshing water to trickle down his back and chest. Finally, he cupped his hands for a drink. The water tasted sweet. He repeated the process four more times. At last, his thirst quenched, he turned over and sat down in the cool shade.

William surveyed his handiwork. The tall, dark-green grasses that he had cut lay horizontally upon the ground where they would dry in the sun. In three days, the dried hay would be ready for stacking. He nodded approvingly. He had done a man's work that morning. His father would be most proud of his progress by day's end.

Despite his feeling of accomplishment, William was very tired. He was a bit hungry, too, but not hungry enough to go back to the house in search of food. Instead, he elected to skip his mid-day meal and take a short nap. He lay back onto the thick, spongy moss that lined the creek bank and almost immediately fell into a deep sleep.

Sometime later, in the midst of his deep slumber, he felt a sharp blow against his boot. He sat upright, greatly startled. His father loomed over him. The man was smiling.

"Are you planning to sleep away the rest of the day?" Will teased playfully.

"I was just about to get up," declared young William, groggily. He stretched. He felt a bit ashamed for being caught asleep in the field. He was so comfortable that he felt as if he could have slept on that cool moss until tomorrow's breakfast. He sat up and then rubbed his sleep-swollen eyes.

"I need you to take a little break from your napping and do something for me ... for Mrs. Garrison, actually."

"Oh?" answered William, his interest piqued. "What, pray tell?"

His father reached inside his coat pocket and removed a small, folded piece of paper. "I need you to go into Camden Town and post this letter for me." He handed it to his son. "John Garrison needs to know about his family. Somehow, he needs to find a way to come home."

"Camden Town?" William exclaimed. "That's eight miles away. Why there?"

"Because you can post the letter by boat there. It will ensure a more rapid delivery. You need only go to the Wateree River docks and locate a vessel headed downstream toward the coast. Post the letter with its captain. He is duty-bound to see it delivered to the authorities in Charlestown." He handed William a silver coin. "This should cover his expense."

William examined the front of the letter. It was addressed, "*Sgt. John Garrison, 1ˢᵗ North Carolina Regiment of the Continental Army – Prisoner at Charlestown.*" On the left side of the folded letter, near the bottom, was written, "*Posted by Boat from Camden Town*."

William was confused. "I thought Mr. Garrison was up in Pennsylvania."

"He was there for over a year, but his regiment moved down south last year. He was one of the defenders at Charlestown when it fell to Clinton and Cornwallis. The entire rebel army was taken prisoner back in the spring. Now, he is in a military prison or, perhaps, on a ship in the harbor there. I have heard that there are hundreds, perhaps thousands, of men now confined to prison ships in Charlestown harbor."

"Ghastly," commented William.

"Indeed." His father nodded grimly.

"But, why is he in the North Carolina Line? Why join a regiment from another colony?"

Will shrugged. "I suppose he was anxious to join in the fight. Being out here amongst so many Loyalist folk left him with few options. There were no South Carolina rebel regiments early in the war. He joined the 1st North Carolina when they took the field in Ninety-Six District in December of 1775. He came home for a while after that, but eventually went back to rejoin the regiment when it went north. He has come back home several times over the years, but always he has returned to the army."

William nodded slightly. That made sense. He held up the letter in his right hand. "Do you think John Garrison will ever get this letter?"

"I pray so. Since he is held prisoner here in South Carolina, I believe he is actually *more* likely to receive it. I doubt that any letter would ever find him if he were in a soldier's encampment up north."

William pointed to the hayfield. "My work is not yet

done here. I was hoping to have all this hay on the ground before nightfall."

"It can wait," his father reassured him. "This task that I am assigning you is far more important than cutting hay. Do you not agree?"

"Of course I do, Father."

"Good. Go, then, and fetch yourself some food from the house. Your mother tells me you have not eaten a bite since breakfast, and she is worried sick. Then, saddle Molly and head on into town with haste. I want you back home for supper."

"Yes, sir," answered William as he stood. "You can count on me."

THE RIDE along the highway to Camden Town was uneventful. Molly seemed to enjoy the journey. She trotted most of the way, allowing William to reach his destination shortly after 2:00 in the afternoon. He rode immediately to the riverbank and then followed a narrow trail that led to the docks where merchants and boats exchanged trade goods. Numerous small vessels and flatboats were anchored nearby or tied to the docks.

William tethered Molly to a small tree near a large patch of green grass. There was ample water for the animal in a nearby trough. He immediately went in search of a boat that would depart for Charlestown within a day. It did not take him long to spot a cargo-laden flatboat tied to the last dock. William learned, after a brief discussion with a dock hand, that the vessel was set to cast off at dawn on the following morning. He was quite relieved. His mission would not take as long as he had feared. All he needed to do now was locate the boat's owner and transfer the letter for delivery.

As William walked down the narrow gangway that led to the boat, he was suddenly confronted by a trio of young men. He knew these fellows well. They were Darby Ellison, Andrew Cutler, and Ferris McClelland, all of them lads from Fairfield District. They lived just a few miles north of Jackson's Creek.

William had grown up with these boys. They had played together often as children. But, as it so often does, life had taken these three on a different path than that of William Newman. These notorious lads were known throughout the region as a poor, hardscrabble, unlawful lot. They were shabbily dressed. Their clothing was filled with holes and streaked with mud and stains. In all likelihood, they were prowling for trouble. William wanted nothing to do with them. And, on this particular day, he had neither the time nor the desire for conversation or foolishness.

"Oy! If it isn't William Newman of the creek!" chirped Darby Ellison, the well-known ringleader of the three ruffians. He eyed William with some disdain. "Little William be dressed up like a fine gentleman, don't he, boys?"

The two other fellows grunted and displayed mischievous grins. "A gentleman, indeed," echoed Ferris McClelland.

The three boys positioned themselves elbow-to-elbow, noticeably blocking the walkway. Surrounded by the waters of the riverbank and his course impeded, William had no choice but to address them.

"Hello, Darby," William declared warily. "It is good to see you fellows, but I have little time for socializing today." He pointed at the flatboat at the end of the dock. "I do not mean to be rude, but I have an important errand on that boat. I must be on my way and with haste. My father requires me home before supper."

"I've been hearing some troubling things about you," announced Darby, pointing his skinny finger at William and ignoring his comments. "Word is you've been cozying up to some rebels out your way."

"We have no rebels out our way," retorted William bluntly.

"That's not what I hear," growled the filthy lad. "People say you and your folk have been giving comfort to the King's enemies."

William's face flushed red and hot. "Well, you have heard wrong, Darby."

Ellison shook his head slowly and made a clicking sound with his mouth. He took a step closer to William. "No, Willie boy, I heard right. You were seen putting them Garrison brats into the ground. And other folks say you have that rebel wench, Agnes Garrison, laying up in your house right now. People hereabouts can't stop talking about it. They all seem mighty disappointed with the Newmans and their treasonous ways."

Rage washed across William. He instinctively clenched both of his hands into fists. The desire to punch Darby Ellison in the face was overwhelming.

"We are not traitors. Mrs. Garrison is no rebel." He inhaled a deep, livid breath. "And neither were her dead children."

"They were the spawn of a rebel fool, and that makes them rebels, as well. Anyhow, you and your folk put them into the ground, did you not?" challenged Darby.

"Of course, we did. We have the decency to help take care of our neighbors, no matter their politics. Indeed, we count it an honor." William spat into the water that flowed alongside the gangway. "I would even put shovel to dirt to bury you, Darby, should I be called upon to do so. I might even enjoy that task."

William's blatant insult struck a nerve in Darby Ellison. The troublemaking youth exclaimed a shout of anger and then immediately lunged at William, his fists swinging. William ducked to his left and avoided the attacker's initial blows. Darby, failing to make contact with his fists, lost his balance. Seizing upon Darby's miscalculation, William gave the staggering boy a quick shove from behind. Instantly, he tumbled face-first off of the gangway and then landed in the muddy water of the river with a huge splash. William grinned in triumph at the sound of Darby's surprised gasp and the sight of his foe disappearing below the surface of the river.

Despite his initial victory, William's triumph was short-lived. Instantly, the other two boys were upon him. Both of them swung wild fists and succeeded in landing several painful blows to William's belly and face. One particularly violent impact knocked the wind out of him. Though he fought valiantly, he was unable to breathe and could not maneuver on the narrow gangway. Before he knew it, the attackers had knocked William down onto his back and then pinned him against the rough, splintery boards of the gangway. Seconds later, the grinning, soaking-wet face of Darby Ellison loomed over him. Drops of water trickled from Darby's chin and splashed onto William's face.

Despite his precarious situation, William could not help but smile at the soaking-wet ruffian. He grunted, "'Tis a fine day for a swim, isn't it, Darby?"

Darby Ellison's smile vanished. Instantly, he lifted his foot and delivered a vicious kick to William's side. The striking of his toe against William's coat tore the linen and ripped his pocket open. A folded piece of paper tumbled out onto the gangway. It was the letter to John Garrison!

"Oy! What's this?" asked Darby, reaching down. He picked up the letter, gave it a quick glance, and then held it toward both of his friends. "'Tis a letter to a rebel soldier! I knew the Newmans were but a pack of rebel scum!"

"That letter is none of your concern, Darby Ellison," William hissed. "It is a private correspondence that I must deliver for posting." He added, "Frankly, I'm surprised that any of you can read it."

Darby gave William another vicious kick in the ribs. He was lifting his leg to deliver yet another when the sounds of heavy footfalls reached their ears. Men were running on the gangway from the shore. William shifted his head to look. He saw that one of the men wore a constable's badge. He wielded a pistol. The other two men carried muskets. He felt a wave of relief. Seconds later, the three men arrived at the scene of the fight.

"What is going on here?" demanded the constable.

The two fellows holding William down on the gangway stood and quickly took a step back. William climbed clumsily to his feet, proudly retrieved his dislodged hat, and then turned to face the men. He did his best to straighten his disheveled clothing.

"Constable, I am William Newman of Jackson's Creek, son of William Newman, Sr., here on family business. I have been attacked by this band of ruffians!"

The constable eyed Darby Ellison and his mates with a measure of disgust. "Darby, I thought I told you and your friends to leave town yesterday. I have had my fill of your troublemaking. You will suffer a night or two in jail for your crimes!"

Darby waved his hands defensively. "Wait one moment,

Constable Martin! You have not heard the entire story." He pointed at William. "This here fellow is a rebel spy."

"I am not!" exclaimed William indignantly.

Darby thrust the letter toward the constable. "Just take a look for yourself. He carries a letter addressed to a rebel imprisoned at Charlestown! I tell you, sir, he is a spy!"

"Wait just a moment!" William pleaded. "Constable, I beg you …"

"Silence!" commanded the constable. He examined the front of the letter. He turned it over and checked the unbroken wax seal. He peered suspiciously at William. "Did you, indeed, carry this?"

"Yes, sir. It is a letter to one of my neighbors. My father instructed me to …"

"Shut your treasonous mouth!" barked the constable.

"But, sir!" pleaded William. "Allow me to explain!"

The constable ignored him. He turned to his two assistants. "Edward, escort Mr. Ellison and his mates to the town limits and set them on the road to Fairfield." He cut an angry glance at the three lawbreakers. "If we see them in Camden Town again, we will shoot them on sight! Andrew, place this other lad in irons and take him to the jail. I will go and inform the magistrate that we have captured a potential spy and enemy of the Crown. Lord willing, we may have us a hanging at dawn tomorrow!"

8

THE MAKING OF A REBEL

With the turn of an ancient key, the iron mechanism clicked inside the giant lock. Hanging his lantern on a nearby nail, the jailer removed the lock from its iron rings and then slowly pulled the heavy doorway open. The rusty hinges groaned from the weight. In the darkness beyond, the jail cell was eerily quiet. Nary a sound came forth.

Will Newman leaned forward and peered into the darkness of the tiny, dank room. He could see nothing. There was no light inside the cell, for there was no window. He wondered if the jailer might somehow be confused. Surely, his son had not been confined inside such a dark, filthy, odorous place.

"Go on, then!" ordered the jailer impatiently. "The young scoundrel is in there, I assure you! Fetch him quickly. I have precious little time to waste on you rebels."

Will shot the scrawny little man a hateful gaze. "We are not rebels, sir."

"Humph!" grunted the jailer. "So say you all."

Will was inclined to strike the man, but he somehow

managed to keep his temper in check. He retorted proudly, "I am Will Newman of Jackson's Creek, a staunch supporter of the Crown and wholeheartedly loyal to my King."

"Of course you are," the man responded sarcastically. "'Tis always the case. No one in this jail is *ever* guilty of treason." He emitted a mocking chuckle.

"My son had best be in a good state of health," Will proclaimed sternly. "For if he is not, it will be *you* who shall stand before the magistrate to answer for *your* crimes."

"Blah, blah, blah!" retorted the obnoxious little man. "Empty threats! I hear them every day from the likes of you." He tapped his foot impatiently. "Well, are you going to claim the lad, or not? I must move another prisoner into this cell. Time is a wastin'!"

Will turned his attention back to the dark, foreboding room. He stepped forward into the blinding darkness. It took a few seconds for his eyes to adjust to the lack of light. At first, he could see nothing at all. After a while, though, his eyes discerned the gray, motionless lump of a human body. Then, suddenly and unexpectedly, the body moved. A weak groan reached Will's ears. Instantly, he recognized the sound of his son's voice!

"William!" he hissed. "I have come to save you, lad!"

William rolled over onto his back. He stared at his father in disbelief. "Papa?" His voice was weak, but it displayed hint of hope. "Papa, is it truly you? Surely, I am dreaming."

Will darted to his son and then knelt beside him. The boy reached a feeble, filthy hand upward to touch his father's face. Will gasped at the horrible state of his son's appearance. His clothing was tattered and torn. His face was bruised. Almost every inch of it was some shade of red, black, or blue. William's left eye was swelled completely shut. His upper lip was split open. Dried blood covered his cheeks and chin.

"It is I, William. No, you are not dreaming. Oh, my son!" his father wailed, heartbroken. "What have they done to you?"

He reached down to take William into his arms. The lad winced from pain when his father touched his shoulder and back.

"It hurts, Papa. They beat me," William groaned. He choked back tears. "They beat me with their fists and with a whip. One man struck me with the stock of his musket."

"I am so very sorry, son. It is all my fault. I should never have sent you here alone."

William shook his head. "It was not your fault, Papa. I have been to Camden Town hundreds of times. But, the authorities here are no longer good men. They are vile and wicked and thirsty for blood. They imagine a rebel behind every blade of grass."

William glanced over his father's shoulder at the jailer. The man stood in the open door and held his lamp high so that the dull glow of the candle filled the cell. His face revealed an evil and almost gleeful grin.

William whispered to his father, "That one is the worst of the lot. He beat me horribly."

"I believe you, Son. You can tell me all about it later. But first, let us flee this horrid place. Can you stand and walk?"

"I believe so. My legs are unhurt, but I am weak. Do you have any water?" he begged through parched lips. "I've had neither food nor water since they put me here. How long has it been? I have lost track of time."

"Three days have passed since your arrest. No, William, I have no water with me now. But, worry not. Soon you will quench your thirst. You are coming with me straightaway. I have secured your release and prepared a room in a nice tavern close by. You will drink, eat, bathe, and rest. Tomorrow, we will appear before the magistrate and make right this unspeakable injustice."

William offered a weak smile. "That sounds good. But, I just want to go home."

"Soon, my boy ... soon. Tomorrow night you will sleep in your own bed and receive care from your mother's hand. I promise you this. Meanwhile, we will make the best of our circumstances here. Now, take hold of my arm. I want you out of this jail."

William nodded. Gripping his father's arm, the two of them strained together. Will managed to lift the lad to his feet. Then, slowly and carefully, he assisted his son out of the cell. Neither of them spoke a word to the jailer as they passed by him.

"Sleep tight, little laddie," the cruel jailer whispered sarcastically. "I'll be seeing you back here in a day or two, I'm sure."

Will and his son ignored the petty little man. They stepped over the threshold and then trudged slowly toward the warm, inviting sunlight that illuminated the far end of the hallway.

∾

The Following Afternoon

WILL and William Newman stood together before the Camden District magistrate. Young William was clad in a fresh, clean suit of brown linen. He looked every bit the gentleman. Indeed, he looked nothing at all like the battered, filthy boy that lay sprawled upon the floor of the jail on the previous day. The only evidence that remained of his recent ordeal shone on his face. Numerous cuts and bruises had begun to morph into various shades of yellow and green, giving evidence of rapid healing. Will Newman, though his demeanor remained dignified, was clearly disgusted and incensed over the circumstances of his son's arrest and treatment.

Impatient, Will cleared his throat and then spoke. "As you can see, Mr. Phillips, there is no hint of sedition in my correspondence. It is merely a private letter in which I sought to inform a neighbor about the deaths of his children. That neighbor just happens to be a rebel prisoner in Charlestown. This letter was unlawfully seized and my son was illegally detained. Furthermore, following his lawless arrest, he was mistreated, deprived of sustenance, and beaten during his captivity. I demand satisfaction for this unthinkable miscarriage of justice!"

The magistrate held up an indignant hand toward Will. "I do not tolerate demands from *anyone* in this hall of justice. That includes you, Mr. Newman. You will remain silent until I finish reading."

The portly, sweaty, red-faced fellow continued to peer intently at the open letter. His lips wagged as he read the words. Will grew more impatient and irritated with each passing second. At long last, it appeared that the magistrate was finished. He handed the letter to Will, then removed his spectacles and dropped them casually onto his desk.

"Though I believe it unwise for you to send a letter to a rebel prisoner in such times as these, I find nothing illegal in it. The information contained here is, indeed, personal in nature. There is no form of political speech nor is there mentioned anything of a sensitive military nature." He cut his eyes toward William. "Young man, you are free to go about your business. As you do, I send you forth with the sincerest apologies of this court and of the Crown. Your case is dismissed and this matter is closed." He motioned to a fellow near the back of the room. "Bring in the next!"

"But, what of the men who beat my son?" Will challenged harshly. "There have been crimes committed against my family. I demand that the guilty men be punished!"

"Ah! There you go again, Mr. Newman. What did I just say regarding the inappropriate nature of demands in my courtroom?" barked the magistrate angrily.

"I beg your pardon, sir," Will responded humbly, bowing slightly at the waist. "Please forgive my emotional state. I am simply saying that something *must* be done to resolve this series of egregious events. Loyal subjects of the King should not be afflicted with false arrest and imprisonment. Is it British justice for a mere lad to be whipped and beaten by the authorities without any evidence of wrongdoing? Is it now the policy of Camden District to withhold food and water from its prisoners? There are many serious issues here that must be addressed."

"And I will address them all in the due course of time," retorted the magistrate coolly. "I certainly do not need *you* to tell me how to do *my* job. Mr. Newman, I would advise you to accept this dismissal gladly and then return peacefully to your home. Take your boy and go. I wish to hear no more of this."

Enraged, Will glowered at the magistrate. He tugged at his son's arm. "Come along, William. Obviously, there is no true justice to be found in this place. We have had our fill of Camden Town. Let us shake off its dust and return home to our peaceful Jackson's Creek."

The Newman men turned and marched proudly toward the exit. As they departed, Will spotted the crooked jailer standing just inside the doorway. The fellow's pompous smirk was gone from his face. He seemed genuinely displeased that young William had been released.

As he passed by the man, Will paused and then declared, "I pray, sir, that we never see one another again. For, if we do, it will be a very bad day for you. I promise you this."

He tugged at William's arm and then urged him through the door and into the street beyond.

~

Three Months Later
Sunday, October 29, 1780

SUNDAY DINNER WAS DONE. It was a cool but pleasant autumn day, and a perfect one for a stroll. About an hour after the noontime meal, William and Mary left their parents sitting on the front porch of the Newman home and headed out toward the eastern pasture. A half-hour later, they were walking arm in arm beside the sparkling, dancing waters of Jackson's Creek. They had walked this familiar pathway together hundreds of times before.

As they approached a familiar stopping place, William motioned toward a sunshine-bathed cluster of low, flat sandstone rocks. "Shall we sit and rest a while?"

Mary nodded and smiled. "Of course, William. You know that this is one of my most favorite places on the creek."

So, they sat. Mary studied the tall pines swaying overhead. William closed his eyes and basked happily in the comfort of the warm sunshine. It was a peaceful, picturesque setting.

Mary observed apprehensively, "We have talked little since the incident in Camden."

William inhaled a deep, thoughtful breath. "No, we have not. There have not been many opportunities. I have missed our conversations."

She placed her hand gently upon his and smiled. "Well, we have a perfect opportunity right now."

William turned to her. He smiled warmly. "What would you like to talk about today?"

She paused thoughtfully. "I want to know what happened to you in Camden. And I want to know what has been on your mind since. I can see that you have changed. Something is different about you. It is painfully obvious that something still troubles you."

William was reluctant to respond. He stared, blank-faced, at the waters of the creek. He appeared to be measuring his words.

"William, please talk to me," she pleaded softly. "You can tell me anything."

"I fear that you may be disappointed in me," William answered cautiously. "I have been thinking of many things since Camden. Most of all, I have struggled with some doubts."

"What manner of doubts?" she inquired, intrigued.

William shrugged. "Doubts about my beliefs and my politics." Hs slowly turned his eyes toward her. "Doubts about my allegiances."

Mary gasped. Quickly, she withdrew her hand from his. "What are you saying, William? Surely, you are not referring to England and our glorious Sovereign, King George!"

William blinked. "Yes, Mary. Yes, I am."

Her face flushed bright red. "You cannot be serious, William. You are simply confused. Yes, that must be it. You are distraught and your mind remains unsettled because of your misfortune in Camden Town. You just need more time to compose your thoughts."

"It was no matter of *'misfortune,'* Mary!" William responded angrily. "That is a very poor word, indeed. I was arrested. I was falsely accused. I was beaten and placed in chains. The authorities deprived me of food and water for three days. It was no misfortune. It was criminal. And it was done to me in the name of King George." William was becoming livid. "They treated me like that with no consideration whatsoever of all that my family has sacrificed and given for King and country. My father served in the King's army. My brother serves him now!" He scowled. "Such absence of justice simply reveals the presence of tyranny."

She gasped again. "What are you saying, William? Have you turned coat? Will you now join with the rebels?"

"I have not decided, yet," he answered frankly. "But, I must confess that I have given it much serious consideration."

Mary shot to her feet. "I simply cannot believe this! How can you say such treasonous things, William? How can you even think of turning your back upon England and the King?"

William stood slowly. He hissed, "Because, from where I sit, it seems that England and her King have turned their backs upon me, Mary. I have received no such ill treatment from any member of the rebel cause. Never. Not once. Yet, my own allies treat me as a criminal."

Mary took a frightened step away from him. "I cannot listen to any more of this treasonous talk. William, I am very sorry for the horrible way in which you were treated in Camden Town. It was horribly, terribly wrong. But now, *you* are in the wrong."

"How can a man be wrong if he is simply searching the convictions of his heart? I must follow my conscience. Believe me, I have never had any desire whatsoever to join in the fight against England. I have not a rebellious bone within me." He inhaled a shaky, emotional breath. "But, if I am a rebel, Mary, it is only because *they* have made me so."

Mary stomped her foot in anger. It was a most unusual display of emotion for her. "William Newman, I love you. Since we were but little children, I have loved you. I have long dreamed of becoming your wife and building a home and family with you here in the backcountry. Our families have always assumed that our future would be together. I believe that *we* have assumed so, as well." She paused. A cloud of dread seemed to loom over her. "But, I cannot be associated with a traitor to the Crown. And I will not marry a turncoat."

Her words stung William's heart. "You mean ... you would choose some faraway king over me? You would choose a government over me?"

Her face flushed an angry crimson. "It seems that *you* have already chosen some faraway rebels in Philadelphia over *me*! Loyalty to England is the price of my affection, William. I consider it but a small price." She eyed him contemptuously. Her hateful glare disturbed him. "I am going home now. Please do not call upon me until you have rightly sorted your thoughts. When your allegiances are once again to King and country, then we can resume the customary activities of our courtship."

She spun on her heels and then marched angrily away from him. William watched her go. It was all that he could do. Nothing that he could say would stop her.

He mumbled softly, "Goodbye, Mary. No matter what, I will always love you."

❧

Three Months Later – February 2, 1781

As USUAL, William did not sleep well. He tossed and turned. He dozed fitfully, awakening often. Such restlessness had plagued him for many months. William knew full-well the cause of his sleeplessness. It was the epic battle of conscience that raged within him.

Many months before, William had made up his mind to join the rebel cause of independence from Great Britain. Yet, he had still not found the personal courage to pack his bags and leave for the war. He knew that such an act of rebellion would devastate his family. It would break his parents' hearts. It would be a terrible insult to his brother, Austin, who now served in the King's militia. And it would, no doubt, result in the persecution and mistreatment of his parents at the hands of their Loyalist "friends" and neighbors. Deep in his mind and heart, William Newman was a young man who was torn between loyalty to family and loyalty to conscience. It was little wonder that he could not sleep at night.

So, William struggled through another restless, cold, winter night. He lay buried beneath a thick layer of wool blankets. He was in the midst of yet another of his fitful, troubling dreams when he was awakened from his shallow sleep by a clamor of voices. It took a moment for him to discern whether the voices were inside his home or somewhere within his mind. Once he was fully awake, he lay still for a moment and listened. Yes ... the voices were real!

William could hear two men speaking excitedly in the parlor. Curious, he tossed back his blankets, climbed silently from his bed, and then crept toward his bedchamber door. He placed his ear against the door and listened. He heard his father's familiar voice. But, to whom was he speaking?

Suddenly, he recognized the other voice. It was John Austin, son of Bartholomew! He was one of Austin's best friends. But, how could John be here? He was serving in the militia with his brother, Austin. He should be deployed afield with the army. How was it possible for him to be here, at Jackson's Creek, and in their home in the middle of a cold winter night?

A sudden pang of dread struck William's heart. He wondered, silently, *"Has something happened to my brother? Good Heavens! Might he be dead?"*

William strained his ears to eavesdrop through the door. Beyond, he heard his father's anxious voice.

"Tell me now, John! What has happened?" demanded Will, his voice cracking. "Has my boy fallen to the guns of enemy?"

John responded, "No, Mr. Newman. I almost wish that were so. If he were dead in the grave, then, at least, he might retain his honor."

"You had best explain yourself, John." Even through the door, William could hear that his father sounded angry and frustrated.

William's heart raced. After a deafeningly quiet, tormenting pause, John spoke again. "Mr. Newman, I regret to inform you that your son has gone over to the enemy. Austin has turned coat and joined the rebels."

"But ... but ... there *must* be some mistake, John!" moaned Will. "Surely, you have misunderstood his actions. Could he not be on some secret mission for his captain?"

"No, sir. There was no mistaking what Austin did. He was captured with me and about twenty other men from the regiment. On the morning after our capture, the rebel officer in command called a formation. We were made to stand there and watch as Austin placed his hand upon a Bible and swore his rebel oath." John became choked with emotion. "Then, he was assigned as my guard during the first half of my march to the rebel prison camp. The last time I saw your son, he appeared quite comfortable and happy amongst the enemy troops."

"But, then you escaped?"

"Yes, sir. I managed to slip away late the next night. Immediately, I began to make my way back home. I needed to tell you what has happened."

There was a very long pause in their conversation. William heard shuffling footsteps. Moments later, he heard the chair near the fireplace give a loud creak as his father sat down.

Once again, Will spoke. "I knew that my son was troubled. He informed me some time ago that he did not intend to continue in the King's militia once his enlistment was done, but I never, in my wildest thoughts, imagined anything like this."

William had heard enough. Silently, he slipped away from the door and returned to his bed. He crawled beneath the warm covers and lay flat on his back. He digested in his mind all that he had just heard. He could scarcely believe it. Austin Newman, his very own brother, had turned coat and joined the rebel army! He had abandoned England and King George! Now, *he* was fighting for the cause of independence. He was a soldier, not for England, but for the United States of America.

At long last, after months of struggle and indecision, William found the courage to take action. If his brother could change sides in this war, then so could he. His heart no longer bore any allegiance to the English. Indeed, he saw nothing in the Crown except tyranny and abuse. Surely, the thirteen colonies would know a better future as the thirteen United States of America.

"I will go," William whispered proudly to himself. "I, too, shall join with the rebels. I will fight alongside my brother."

He rolled over onto his side and faced the wall, but he was too excited to sleep. Instead, he lay awake and made plans for his departure. It would take him a few days to prepare. In the meantime, he had to figure out a way to break his news to his father.

~

Three Days Later

WILLIAM SAT ATOP HIS HORSE, Molly. His knapsack and saddlebags were packed and bulging with food and supplies. His father stood nearby. Will gazed mournfully at his son.

"I do wish that you would reconsider, William. This is such a drastic decision. Once you take up arms against the King, it cannot be undone."

"I must follow my conscience, Father ... just as you do ... just as Austin did. I only ask that you respect my decision."

"I do respect your decision, Son. But, that does not mean that I have to like it. I realize that you are now a man. You have a mind of your own and you must live according to your convictions. Still, I will miss you terribly. This house will be empty without you." He paused and appeared to choke back a sob. "And your mother and I will worry over you endlessly."

The mention of his mother caused William a measure of regret. "Would Mother not come to see me off?"

Will shook his head. "No, son. She could not bear it. Her heart is broken. But, it does not mean that she loves you any less. She will pray for you every single day, as will I."

"I know. Please pray, also, for my cause."

Will grimaced. "Son, I do not believe that your mother nor I are quite ready for that. But, you are our son, no matter your politics. We will love you without condition and pray fervently for your health and for your safe return."

"That will have to do, then, I suppose." William glanced toward the road. "Well, I'd best be going. I have a long day's journey ahead of me."

"Travel safely. Keep an eye out for strangers," cautioned Will. He patted his boy on the knee. His eyes twinkled. "Take care of yourself, you little turncoat. Please come back to us."

William grinned. "I will, Papa. I promise."

There was nothing else to say. William clucked at his horse and then turned her toward the northwest. Without looking back, he rode away from his parents and his home. He rode toward the great conflict that would one day be known as the American Revolution.

PART III

I FIGHT FOR FREEDOM

9

BECOMING A SOLDIER

February 18, 1781

William had no idea that finding the South Carolina militia would be such a difficult task. He was looking for the encampment of General Thomas Sumpter, commander of the American forces in South Carolina. But, General Sumpter was proving hard to find. It made sense, actually. With all of the divided loyalties in the South Carolina backcountry, a shrewd commander would do well to keep the location of his encampment secret.

As he traveled north from Camden, William encountered fewer and fewer friendly folk. Most of the frontier settlers were not inclined to share intelligence and information with a stranger. It seemed that the further he traveled, the more suspicious the people became. Though William made numerous inquiries at homesteads and plantations, no one would answer his questions. Indeed, some even slammed their doors in his face at the mere mention of General Sumpter.

He was almost ready to quit and return home when, at long last, he discovered what he was looking for. William had stopped for the night at a backcountry tavern about twenty miles north of Camden Town. Over breakfast, the curious and talkative owner of the tavern engaged him in friendly conversation. Once he became convinced of the lad's earnest desire to join the Patriot army, he revealed the location of General Thomas Sumpter's militia encampment. It was on the banks of the Catawba River, up near the border with North Carolina. William was, indeed, headed in the right direction. With good weather and a little luck, he could reach the encampment in less than two days.

Excited by the news and well-rested from a comfortable night's sleep at the warm tavern, William departed immediately. He guided his mare northwest, traveling cross-country. He skirted about a dozen small farms, careful to avoid being spotted. He did not want to arouse any unwanted attention. He crossed two large streams and a myriad of small creeks and ditches. Around mid-morning, he reached the Great Philadelphia Wagon Road. This well-traveled highway, true to its name, meandered northward through North Carolina and Virginia and reached all the way to the great city of Philadelphia in Pennsylvania.

The wagon road followed an ancient route known as the Great Warrior's Trading Path, or the Catawba Path. It was an eons-old trade route used by the Catawbas and countless other native tribes long before the Europeans came. In recent years, however, it had served a much different purpose. Now, the oft-traveled, dusty road brought thousands of Scotch-Irish settlers down from the north into the Carolina backcountry. More and more pioneers followed this route southward each summer. Most came in search of farmland and a quiet country far from overcrowded cities.

William assumed that the road would take him in the general direction of the encampment. It would also help him reach his destination more quickly. Before taking the road, however, he first had to scout it for any potential danger. He paused on a slight rise on the eastern side of the highway. Wisely, he concealed himself in a small thicket of brush and low trees and surveyed the landscape. He peered in both directions along the roadway, listening intently for the telltale sounds of travelers. There were none.

Several minutes later, satisfied that all was quiet and that it was safe to use the road, he clucked at Molly and gave the reins a gentle tug toward the right. The horse snorted eagerly, stepped out of the brush, and then eased down the low embankment onto the roadway. Starting at an easy trot, the mare quickly found her speed and eased into a pleasant canter.

The road was hard-packed and smooth, so William made good time. Though it was winter, the weather was pleasantly warm for February and perfect for journeying. He encountered only two other travelers and avoided both without incident. The miles passed quickly. He rode for about three hours and then stopped shortly after noon, resting his horse in the shade of a tall stand of pines that lay about fifty yards east of the road. There was a small, clear pond near the pines that provided ample clean, fresh water. He ate a light meal of jerked venison and cold corn cakes and rewarded Molly with a small sack of tasty, sweet oats.

As William rested, his mind wandered. His head was filled with many burning questions. Would he find any friends at the encampment? Would his brother, Austin, be there? What would it be like to serve in the army? Would he ever be in a battle? If so, would he be brave in the face of the enemy?

His belly full, William leaned back against the rough bark of a pine tree and closed his eyes. His fowling gun lay across his lap and at the ready. He knew that he needed to get moving once again, but it had already been a long and tiring day of travel. A short rest was definitely in order, especially for Molly. She was a farm horse, and not entirely accustomed to traveling such long distances. Truth be told, William was not used to such long travel, either. He needed the rest.

Though he had not intended to doze, William drifted into a light, dreamless sleep. Actually, he was not entirely asleep. He hovered somewhere in that mysterious place between the waking and slumbering worlds. His mind slept, yet he still remained somewhat aware of his surroundings.

Suddenly, Molly gave a snort. The horse's unexpected alert yanked William from his dozing. He immediately opened his eyes. He sat upright quickly and then peered toward the mare. Curiously, Molly seemed to be staring directly through him. He began to turn and look behind him when a dull, metallic click caused him to freeze in place. It was the unmistakable sound of a flintlock being cocked.

"Easy there, lad," growled a low, grizzled voice. "Easy now. Turn around and face me ... nice and slow. Don't even think about touching your gun. Keep your hands where I can see them."

William lifted his hands high and then slowly turned. Ten paces away, three men stood glaring at him. The one in the center held a musket pointed squarely at William's chest. The other two held their muskets at the ready. They appeared to be hard men. Their black felt cocked hats were stained and bleached by sun and rain. Their coats, breeches, and buckskin leggings were filthy. Clearly, these men had been in the field for a long time.

"And just who might you be?" inquired the man who was pointing the musket at him. "'Tis odd to find a lad lounging about in the trees. Are you a spy or lookout, perhaps? Are you keeping watch over this road?"

One of the other men spat on the ground. "Well, iff'n he is, he ain't doin' a very good job of it. Sleepin' on watch gets a man shot by the firin' squad. Maybe we ought to save his captain the trouble." The fellow pulled back the hammer on his musket.

"Shut your mouth, Jeb," growled the man in the middle. Clearly, he was in charge of the group. He glared at William. "Speak, boy. Who is your commander? Where is your regiment?"

William gulped nervously. "I have no commander, for I serve in no army. I am William Newman of the Fairfield District."

The fellow in charge eyed him with an air of suspicion. "You are a far piece from home, lad. Why are you out here in the backcountry all by yourself? And why are you sleeping in the middle of the afternoon with no one to keep watch? There is a war hereabouts, you know."

"Yes, I know," William answered. "I left home a few days ago. I am traveling north in search of ..." he paused cautiously, "... in search of some friends."

"What manner of friends?" hissed the man. "You had best explain yourself, boy!"

William was outside his mind with worry and fear. Should he reveal his intentions of joining the rebel militia? What if these men were Loyalists? Surely, if they were servants of King George, they would string him up from the nearest limb! His mind raced. How could he diffuse this dangerous situation? He needed to stall and glean more information from them.

"May I lower my hands, please? My arms are aching."

The fellow paused a moment, then glanced at the man to his right. "Get his fowler, Jeb. And check him for pistols and blades. He is a runt of a lad, but he could still kill one of us if we're not careful."

The man named Jeb leaned his own musket against a tree and then proceeded cautiously toward William. He grabbed the stock of William's fowling gun and then tossed it aside. Quickly, he pulled William's coat open and checked his belt. He removed William's hunting knife, tucking it away inside his own belt. He patted the boy's coat pockets and checked inside the tops of his wool leggings.

"He is disarmed," announced Jeb. "No pistols. His only knife is an old skinning blade, and a rusty one, to boot."

"Good," answered the fellow with the musket. He motioned with the barrel for William to stand. William complied. "Now, keep talking, boy. What is your purpose here? You are way too far from home to be out hunting. Tell me now. I have little time to waste."

Attempting to ease the discomfort, William coaxed the muscles in his face to form a friendly smile. He asked cautiously, "If I were to say to you, 'God save King George,' would you approve or disapprove?"

The man's face twisted into an angry scowl. His eyes narrowed. "Well, lad, I do not think that I would approve of that, at all. Not one bit, in fact."

William's face relaxed. His smile instantly transformed into a genuine one. He exclaimed, "What a relief, indeed!"

The musket-wielding man appeared somewhat confused.

William explained, "Sir, I am traveling northward in

search of General Sumpter's encampment. My older brother has recently joined your cause. I simply want to locate my brother and my district's regiment and join them."

"You intend to join the cause for independency?" the man clarified. "You would fight against the Tories and the Lobsterbacks?"

William nodded. His face displayed determination. "I would, indeed."

The man lowered his musket slowly. "Newman, you say?" He thought for a moment. He cut his eyes at the fellow named Jeb. "Wasn't there a Newman fellow who turned coat and joined us right after the fight at Cowpens?"

Jeb nodded. "I remember it well. Everyone was talkin' about it. He swore his oath right there in front of his Tory friends. 'Twas a sight to behold."

The other fellow added, "I remember, also. I know him. Austin Newman is his name. He serves under Colonel Winn in the Fairfield Regiment."

"Austin is my brother!" exclaimed William. "Colonel Richard Winn is a neighbor and a personal friend of my father's. Oh, what good fortune! I have been searching for the army and now you gentlemen have found me!"

Suspicion evaporated from the soldier's face as he cradled his musket comfortably in the crook of his left arm. "Well, I reckon you've been on the right trail, lad. We are scouts for General Sumpter's army, tasked with finding an encampment site for tonight." He glanced around the area and then pointed to the pond. "This looks like as good a place as any. It appears to have clean water."

William's eyes widened with surprise. "General Sumpter is near?"

The man nodded. "He is about three miles north. We are scouting ahead for his force. We have around three hundred men. We are moving south to attack a Tory outpost in the Orangeburgh District." He stepped forward and extended a friendly hand to William. "I am Captain James Venable of the New Acquisition District Regiment." He turned to the man who had searched and disarmed William. "Jeb, go back and inform the general that we have located a fine place to camp. We will survey and prepare the area and await his arrival."

Jeb nodded. "Yes, sir." He turned and then trudged northward. He quickly disappeared through the thick forest of pines.

William's heart raced with excitement. "Captain, is my brother traveling with you?"

Captain Venable shook his head. "I have no idea. He could be. We have a couple of companies from Fairfield District. Colonel Winn is leading them." He grinned. "Whether he is deployed with us now or not, you should reunite with your brother soon. I am certain that one of the captains from Fairfield will be glad to have you join his company. If not, come and find me before nightfall. I will make a place for you in mine." He nodded toward William's horse. "That mare of yours looks to be a fine animal, and I could definitely use a scout on horseback."

William was elated. "Yes, sir! I will."

"Good," responded Captain Venable, nodding. "Now, Private Newman, in less than two hours, these woods will be occupied by three hundred tired and hungry men. 'Twill be a cold night, and they will need wood for their cooking fires. Can you begin gathering firewood for your comrades?"

"Yes, sir!"

William, filled with excitement and energy, took to the woods in search of fuel for the army's fires. He could scarcely believe it! He was now a Patriot and soldier of the United States of America!

Sumpter's Encampment - Shortly After Dark

COLONEL RICHARD WINN rose from his comfortable folding chair beside his campfire and stepped forward to greet William. He offered the lad a warm smile and an excited handshake.

"Little William Newman!" he exclaimed. "As I live and breathe! Good heavens! You are not so little anymore. What has your mother been feeding you? The last time I saw you, your head came only to my waist."

"It has been a few years, sir," acknowledged William. "But, it is truly good to see you again."

"What on earth are you doing here? Come. Sit with me for a spell." The colonel motioned to a large log that lay beside his campfire.

"Thank you, Mr. Winn." He sat down on the log. The colonel returned to his seat on the opposite side of the toasty fire.

William explained, "I came here to join your regiment, sir. It is time for me to get into this fight."

"So, then ... you have decided to follow in your brother's footsteps?"

"Yes, sir. We received word some weeks ago that Austin had turned coat and joined your regiment. I must confess that I, too, had been struggling with such a decision for quite some time. News of his defection gave me the courage to do the same."

"What about your father?" asked the colonel. His gaze

displayed a measure of hopefulness. "Is Will Newman on our side now? Goodness knows I could use an old soldier like him."

William chuckled. "No, sir. Not yet. Papa remains loyal to King George. But, I still hope that he will come around, and soon."

"Well, I shall join you in this hope," Colonel Winn promised.

There was a pause in their conversation. William's face betrayed a feeling of disappointment. "I had hoped to find Austin here with you today. But, I have searched the entire encampment since your arrival and have seen no sign of him."

Colonel Winn shook his head regretfully. "You just missed him, I am afraid. There was an outbreak of the flux in his company. To be sure, it was a situation that threatened the entire regiment. For everyone's safety, I thought it best to empty their camp. I granted leave to all of the men who serve in Captain Mitchell's company and the company encamped near to them. That was two days ago. My guess is that Austin is probably home by now."

"Was he ill when he departed?" asked William, greatly concerned.

"No. He was healthy and in good spirits, as were most of his comrades. He will report back to camp in a few weeks. No doubt he will be much fatter and happier after several days of your lovely mother's fine cooking."

William grinned at the thought. However, almost immediately his chin dropped to his chest. It was heartbreaking to know that he had missed seeing Austin by a mere two days.

"Do not despair, young William. You will see your big brother in a few weeks. In the meantime, I am starved for news from home. Tell me, what has occurred in recent days back in the district? How are things on the banks of the lovely Jackson's Creek?"

William shrugged. "There is much to tell. Honestly, I do not know where to start."

"Well, just begin with the circumstances that brought you here. What compelled you to go against the politics of your father and join our cause?"

With that open invitation, William began the story of his personal journey of change. He described in great detail the attack upon the Garrison farm and the deaths of all of the children in the home. He expressed his utter disappointment in his Tory neighbors for abandoning the Garrisons in their time of need. He told of his experiences in Camden when he was arrested and beaten for attempting to post a letter to John Garrison at his prison in Charlestown. Finally, he explained how he learned of Austin's abandoning the Loyalist cause and joining the American militia.

Colonel Winn offered neither comment nor question throughout William's long and sometimes emotional discourse. He simply sat and listened. Occasionally, he would toss a log onto the campfire or poke at the coals of the fire with a long stick. He appeared to be digesting all of the lad's words. It took William almost a half-hour to give his entire account. Finally, when he had nothing else to say, he just sat and stared into the fire. After a rather long time of silence, the colonel spoke.

"I heard about the attack on the Garrison farm. That was a ghastly affair, indeed. Such injustices are far too common out here on the frontier these days. But, they are symptoms of the bloody, violent war in which we now engage, William. Ours is, in every sense of the word, a civil war. It is neighbor against neighbor. In your case, it is now even father against son."

"Oh, I will *never* take up arms against my father!" William declared adamantly.

"Of course you won't, William. And I would never order you to do so. But, for now, you do stand in opposition to one another. He supports King George and England. You have come here to fight and expel King George's troops from our lands and shores. 'Tis no small thing, is it?"

William shook his head grimly. "No sir, it is not. It is a very big thing, indeed. Perhaps that it why it took me so long to act upon my convictions."

"And that makes the story of your personal journey all the more amazing." Colonel Winn rose to his feet. William stood, as well. "You have had a change of heart and mind. Now, I will take part in the changing of your body. Right now, you are just a little turncoat. But I am going to turn you into a soldier."

"I would be most honored to serve in your regiment, sir." He grinned. "But, if you do not need me, Captain Venable did offer me a place in his company."

Colonel Winn growled in disgust. "I will not allow it! Let those New Acquisition folk recruit for their own militia. You are Fairfield District, and you will serve with me. Now, tell me, did you come on foot or on horseback?"

"I rode Molly, my mare."

Colonel Winn nodded. "I remember that horse. She's a fine animal, as best I recall."

"She is, indeed, sir."

Just at that moment, a gentleman approached from the direction of the soldier encampment. He tipped his hat to the colonel. "Begging your pardon, and sorry for the interruption, sir. Our men are all accounted for and secure in the camp. We shall bed down within the hour."

"Very good, Captain Turner." The colonel nodded

toward William. "John, do you know William Newman from Jackson's Creek?"

"Will Newman's boy?" asked the captain. "The Tory?"

The colonel nodded. "And younger brother to Austin Newman, of Captain Mitchell's company." He glanced at William. "John, I am assigning this new recruit to your company. He came in on a fine horse. Since you have no mounted scouts, I assume that you can use him."

The captain raised an eyebrow in surprise. "That I can, sir. Immediately so."

"Very good. I will record the enlistment of William Newman in my ledger tonight and add him to your company muster roll. He shall be along shortly. Can you assign him a tent-mate?"

Captain Turner smiled. "I think we can find a spot for him. It does not appear that he will take up much room."

"Excellent," responded the colonel. "You are dismissed, Captain."

Captain Turner tipped his hat respectfully and then headed back toward his company's campfire.

William stood awkwardly for a moment, not sure what to do. Finally, he asked, "Is there anything else you need from me, sir?"

"I do not think so." He paused. "I assume that you brought a weapon from home?"

"Yes, sir. I brought my fowler gun and a knife."

The colonel grimaced. "That will not do, at all ... not for a mounted scout. Do you know how to use a pistol?"

"Yes, sir. Papa has two. I have shot them dozens of times."

"Good. I will have Captain Turner issue you two pistols tomorrow. Someone else can carry your fowling gun, or we can keep it in our munitions wagon. You can get it back when hostilities have ceased. Does that suit you?"

"Yes, sir," William chirped excitedly.

"Very well. Go along then, son. Fetch your horse and then join the captain in his camp. There will be shelter and hot food for you there. Eat plenty. It may be a while before we again enjoy the leisure of a hot meal."

"Yes, sir." William turned to walk away, then paused and spun around to face the colonel. "Colonel Winn, is there a battle coming? Will we fight the enemy tomorrow?"

The officer nodded grimly. "Yes, Private Newman. There is a battle brewing in the south. I believe we *will* meet the enemy tomorrow."

10

WILLIAM'S BATTLE

February 20, 1781
Early Evening

The evening was quiet. All shooting had ceased. There was a pause in the siege of Fort Granby. The Tories inside the fort were quiet. All along the Patriot lines men rested. Some cooked meager meals over small campfires. Others relaxed, smoked their clay pipes, and talked. Near the far right end of the line there came the unmistakable whine of a fiddle as a talented soldier played a familiar tune for his mates.

William Newman was relaxing near his own campfire alongside a fellow named Thomas Nelson. Thomas was a boyhood friend of William's. They lived only three miles apart back in the Fairfield District. Thomas had been serving in Colonel Winn's regiment for almost three months. William was thrilled to discover an old friend in the regiment. The young men had been inseparable since William's arrival in camp.

Thomas pointed at three odd-looking contraptions

sitting in the adjacent field. He snickered mockingly. "Did you ever reckon those silly things would actually work?"

"There was a chance, I suppose," William answered, chuckling and shaking his head. "Though, I rather think it was a slim chance. My guess is that someone inside the fort had a spyglass. No doubt they could tell the difference between iron cannons and painted pine logs."

The objects of their discussion were three hastily-constructed "Quaker cannons." But, in truth, they were not cannons, at all. They were actually fake pieces of artillery, constructed from appropriately-sized pine logs, painted black, and then suspended between two wagon wheels. From a long distance they bore a remote resemblance to cannons. But, up close, it was clear that they were not.

General Sumpter's strategy had been simple. He had hoped to use the fake cannons to bluff the Loyalist commander of the besieged Fort Granby into surrendering his post. Earlier in the afternoon, pretend artillerymen rolled the three counterfeit cannons into the edge of the field, far away from the fort, but still visible to the men inside. General Sumpter then sent messengers under the white flag of parley to demand the fort's surrender. He promised the enemy commander that, without his immediate surrender, he would open fire on the fort with his three deadly artillery cannons. He hinted that his big guns would reduce the walls and buildings of their fort into splinters.

Unfortunately for the Americans, the general's ruse did not work. The Loyalist commander, Major Andrew Maxwell of Maryland, called Sumpter's bluff and refused to surrender. The Tories remained concealed inside their fortress walls. Instead of surrendering, they demonstrated their resolve by returning intense fire against the attackers.

It was yet another humiliating failure for General Sumpter.

The object of the American attack was called Fort Granby by the British, but local folk had always called it Fort Congaree. The structure was well-constructed and well-defended. It was protected to the east and northeast by the deep waters of the Congaree River. All other sides of the outpost had tall palisades and were protected by deep ditches and earth berms. The only approach to the fort was through wide-open fields, placing attackers under constant fire from the fort's defenders.

The initial assault by the American force on the previous morning had been repulsed quickly and easily by the Tories. After that failed assault, General Sumpter ordered that continuous rifle and musket fire be brought to bear on the enemy. Though ineffective, the small arms fire kept the defenders pinned down behind cover while the Patriot carpenters began construction of their "Quaker cannons."

Thus, every effort by General Sumpter to take the fort, including his fake artillery, had failed. Now, after almost thirty-six hours of laying siege upon the fort, things remained exactly as they were before the American force arrived. The Americans remained behind cover in the distant woods. The "Quaker cannons" sat dead in a pasture. The Tories still held the fort and controlled the river. And General Sumpter, ever an impatient man, was becoming more and more angry and frustrated.

"Reckon what General Sumpter will do next?" wondered Thomas. "It appears to me that, without any cannons, there's no way we can ever take that fort. These Tories are dug in to stay."

"I fear you may be right," William agreed. "And from

where I sit, it has not been much of a battle at all." He patted the pistol in his belt. "There has been little work for mounted scouts around here. I have yet to fire a single shot."

"Really?" Thomas responded in disbelief. He patted his old, rusty fowler. "I've been wasting powder and lead all the long day. All I did was knock a few dents in those palisades." He grunted sarcastically. "Though, I doubt many of my bullets even reached that far. We are a long distance away from those walls."

Suddenly, a voice called from some distance away, "Private Newman! Private William Newman! Where are you?"

William instantly recognized the voice of Captain John Turner, his commanding officer. "Over here, Captain!" he answered.

Captain Turner soon appeared out of the darkness. William and Thomas both jumped to their feet out of respect.

"Sit down, boys. No need for you to get up," the captain urged. "I will join you by your fire. The cold has a bit of a bite to it tonight. I could use some warming."

"Would you like some hot coffee to warm your insides, sir?" Thomas offered.

The captain grinned. "Indeed. I would love some."

Thomas busied himself pouring the captain a cup of hot coffee. Captain Turner sat on the opposite side of the fire from William, leaned against a fallen log, and then removed his hat. He rested the weathered, stained cocked hat on his knee.

"Is this a social call or an official call?" asked William, curious.

"Official, I am afraid. The colonel has assigned you an important mission, Private Newman."

William's heart raced with pride and excitement. "Indeed? Must I go now?"

Thomas interrupted their conversation as he handed the captain a cup of fresh, steaming coffee. "Here you go, sir."

"Thank you, Thomas." Captain Turner turned his attention back to William. "No, William. You mission is scheduled for first light tomorrow. Do you know Bill Gresham, the young fellow from Captain Samuel Lacey's company? I believe he is about your age."

William nodded. "I know Bill, but not very well. We are merely acquainted. I met him at a church event several years ago and have seen him but a few times since."

"Well, you shall know him better after tomorrow. He is a mounted scout for Captain Lacey. Colonel Winn is ordering the two of you to go out together on a long-range patrol."

"Where will we go?"

"You are to head north along the river. You are familiar with the area, are you not?"

"Yes, sir. I have hunted along this river with my father many times. We are but a day's ride southwest from my home."

"Good. Colonel Winn surmised that you would be the right man for this mission. With the stalemate here, General Sumpter fears that reinforcements may be dispatched from Camden. Surely, word of our attack has reached the ears of the British. A relief column could cut off our only line of retreat back to the north. We do not want to get caught in the open on the western side of the Congaree River. Luckily, we know the only place where an army from Camden might cross is at the crossing about eight miles north."

"The sand bar where we crossed two days ago?" William clarified.

"Yes. If the Redcoats come from Camden, that will be their approach. The general wants eyes on that crossing."

"So, then, we are simply to keep watch?"

"Exactly." The captain took a gulp of his coffee. "And if you see any sign of the enemy, you are to return with haste and make your report. Such an event would, no doubt, lead to our immediate retreat." He stood and then quickly downed the remainder of his coffee. "Report to the command tent one hour before sunup. You will receive rations and further instructions at that time. Understood?"

"Yes, sir."

"Outstanding. I will see you in the morning." The captain handed Thomas his empty cup. "Excellent coffee, Mr. Nelson. Nice and strong. I may be back for some more tomorrow."

"I shall have it prepared, sir." Thomas grinned happily.

Captain Turner tipped his hat to the lads. "Gentlemen."

"Good night, sir," both fellows responded in unison.

After the captain disappeared from sight, Thomas gave William a playful nudge. "It looks like you might get a chance to shoot that shiny pistol tomorrow."

William frowned thoughtfully, paused, then declared, "I hope not."

∽

Mid-Morning – The Next Day
Eight Miles North of Fort Granby

WILLIAM PULLED his collar tightly against his neck. A wave of cold air and howling winds invaded the area overnight. The biting winter wind was brutally cold. The sky was gray with an overcast of low clouds. After almost a month of pleasant temperatures, it seemed that winter had finally descended upon the Carolina backcountry.

Holding Molly's reins loosely in his left hand, he walked slowly toward the muddy, sandy riverbank. The Congaree was all of a hundred yards wide at this point. A long sand-bar, almost twenty feet in width, protruded from the western bank where he stood and reached almost all the way across the river. Near the far bank there was a thirty-foot expanse of shallow, slow-moving water. It would barely reach to the height of a man's knees. The narrow road beyond led to the east. It was a perfect place for an army to cross the river.

"Do you see any sign of man or beast?" Bill Gresham asked nervously. He remained mounted on his horse and kept a cautious eye on the distant riverbank.

"Nothing but deer and bird tracks," William answered. "Only the beasts of the forest. I see no sign of men, horses, or wagons."

Bill looked relieved. "Good. The Redcoats have not been here. What do we do now?"

"We follow our orders. We stay here and watch this crossing until dark. If we do not see the enemy by then, we return and make our report to Colonel Winn."

"It is horribly cold," remarked Bill. He cupped his hands in front of his mouth and exhaled the warm air from his lungs in an effort to warm his palms. "We need a fire."

William shook his head slowly. "A fire is risky."

Bill pointed at a stand of thick pines about three hundred yards to their west. "We can hide in those pines and build a small fire. It has not rained for days, so there should be plenty of dry fuel lying about. Old, dry wood will not make much smoke."

William rubbed his cold hands vigorously against the

lapel of his thick wool coat. Bill was right. It was cold, and it seemed to be getting colder. They needed a fire. The air smelled wet. He would not be surprised if they saw rain or even snow in the afternoon or overnight. Winter precipitation was rare in their part of the country, but it still fell from time to time. They needed to prepare for the possibility.

William nodded. "That sounds like a good plan. We can build a small lean-to beneath the pines to block the wind and make maximum use of our fire. If we're lucky, we can rustle up a rabbit or turkey to roast. I could sure use some meat. I didn't have any yesterday. I do not think that I will survive on these meager army rations."

"Won't a gunshot alert the enemy of our presence?" Bill sounded nervous.

William shrugged. "Men hunt in the backcountry all the time. I doubt that a single gunshot or two will stir much suspicion." He pointed at the two pistols in Bill's belt. "Keep a ball in your pistols, for safety's sake. Load birdshot in your fowler for hunting. Then, head over to the pines and get to work on our fire and shelter."

"What are you going to do?"

William angled his head toward the east. "I am going to cross the river and then head down the trail toward Camden for a few miles. Once I see that the way is clear, I will turn back."

"Sounds good," Bill agreed.

William hooked his left foot in the stirrup and nimbly climbed into the saddle atop Molly. "I will be back in a couple of hours. If you hear any shooting from my direction, you will know there is trouble."

Bill nodded. "I will get to work on our shelter and rustle us up some supper."

One Hour Later

WILLIAM, sitting comfortably atop his horse, observed the rutted dirt road that led toward Camden Town. The road wound around the southern edge of a dense forest. Meadows and cultivated fields lay to the right of the road. He was in a good spot for maintaining watch. His position was on a slight rise just inside the edge of a large pine forest, and he could see for almost a mile.

The silence of the afternoon was interrupted by the loud report of a shot far to the west. Soon, another shot cracked. William smiled. It was Bill firing his fowling gun. No doubt his comrade had found some wild game. There would be fresh meat for their supper.

"I hope that was a turkey," he announced out loud. "I have a hankering for some roasted fowl."

Molly, thinking that he was talking to her, gave a happy snort. William chuckled and patted her neck. Suddenly, the mare's ears twitched and alerted. She stared curiously toward the east.

"What is it, girl? Did you hear something?"

William angled his head slightly to the right and listened. He thought that he heard something, as well. But what was it? He focused his mind on the distant sound as he attempted to filter out the ordinary noises of the surrounding forest. Then came the unmistakable sound of a human voice. It was high-pitched and loud. His heart leapt within his chest. But, who was it? And why would they be yelling?

He clucked at his horse and then guided her to the right. He wanted to find better cover deeper inside the pines. He led Molly about thirty yards deeper into the trees and then faced her back toward the east. Peering through the trunks of the trees, he watched the road far to the east. He fixed his eyes on the point where the road appeared from behind a thicket of dense brush.

The voice grew louder. Then came the sounds of other voices. Moments later, men appeared around the bend in the road. There were six riders on horseback. They appeared to be militia. No doubt, they were the forward scouts for a larger infantry force. Soon, William could hear the heavy footfalls of men upon the hard road. The noise was loud and throbbing. The men were marching in formation.

"Molly, how many must there be?" he wondered aloud.

She snorted. Again, her ears twitched. She, too, was watching the approaching riders with cautious curiosity. She pawed at the ground and appeared anxious to go.

"We cannot leave yet, old girl. We have to know how many there are."

Moments later, a throng of scarlet-clad marching soldiers appeared around the bend. William's heart skipped a beat. They were British Regulars! Wave after wave of scarlet-coated infantrymen marched around the bend and maintained their course westward. They were marching in the direction of the river crossing. William remained hidden in the trees as he attempted to discern the number of soldiers. He stopped counting at five hundred. Still, more Redcoats came. The formation of men seemed endless. Following the infantry were roughly two hundred mounted cavalrymen. It was an imposing army, indeed.

"Good Heavens!" he proclaimed. "It must be the entire British army now out of Camden! Let us go, Molly. We must get back and warn our friends!"

William yanked his horse's reins to the right and then gave her a swift kick with his heels. Molly gave a mighty lurch and instantly took off running. Her powerful hooves dug deep into the soft, pine needle-covered ground, flinging soil and debris high into the air. Quickly, she found her pace and then broke into an all-out gallop. It was almost as if the horse understood the urgency of the situation.

Suddenly, there came a shout from amongst the distant British soldiers along the roadway. Men were pointing toward the place in the pines where William had been concealing himself. Someone had spotted his movement. Instantly, a shot rang out! Seconds later, William heard the dull hiss of a lead ball as it flew harmlessly past him and then slammed with a dull thud into a pine trunk. He was way too far out of range to be in any danger. Still, a stray bullet could kill just as easily as a well-aimed one.

"They have seen us! Go, Molly!"

William, an experienced rider, dug his heels deep into his stirrups and held tight. Molly responded to the emotion of her master. She lowered her head and lengthened her strides. She instinctively cut back and forth, weaving her way through the thick trees, yet never missing a step. Clearly, the horse was relishing the thrill of the chase.

But William was not experiencing the same thrill as his trusty mount. He knew all too well that this was no simple chase. He was frightened. He was worried. This was a race for his very life and for the lives of his fellow soldiers.

BILL GRESHAM WAS KNEELING beside his warm fire, anxious for the return of his compatriot. He had already constructed a small, comfortable lean-to shelter. The tiny structure was doing a fine job of blocking the biting northerly wind. The featherless carcass of a medium-sized young turkey dangled loosely on a spit over his fire.

He was quite pleased with himself. The turkey would make for a fine meal. He and William would have a good place to remain warm and dry throughout the increasingly cold winter afternoon. Indeed, his shelter was so well-constructed that the two lads could camp there for the night if they were required to do so.

The sudden report of a gunshot invaded the peace of his cozy shelter. It came from far to the east, somewhere across the river. Bill rose and walked to the edge of the trees. He stared toward the east, remembering William's warning that a gunshot meant trouble for them. There was silence for almost fifteen minutes. He was about to return to his cooking when he heard another shot. Then there were three more!

"What the devil?" he hissed, grabbing his fowler from the place where it rested against a pine tree. He sprinted down the knoll toward the river.

Suddenly, a horse and rider erupted from the dense trees on the far side of the water. It was William! The lad pointed his horse toward the crossing. The mare leapt from the riverbank and landed in the shallow water near the sandbar. Throwing huge waves of spray into the air, she galloped through the water and then quickly found her footing on the sandbar. Horse and rider were soon across. William stopped at the edge of the water to allow his horse a drink. Molly gulped the muddy water thirstily.

Bill was disturbed by the condition of both horse and rider. William appeared frantic. He was out of breath and constantly looking over his shoulder toward the far side of the river. Molly, despite the winter cold, was soaked with sweat. The old girl appeared to be almost spent. William guided his horse away from the water and up onto the embankment. Bill grabbed Molly by the bridle and rubbed a soothing hand across her nose and cheeks.

"What is wrong, William? Is someone chasing you?"

William nodded. He, too, was winded. He retrieved his canteen and took a quick drink of water. He then took a deep breath as he attempted to calm himself. Finally, he burst out, "British cavalrymen! Ten or twelve of them!"

Bill's eyes grew wide with surprise and fear. "Are they alone?"

"Not hardly. The Regulars are out of Camden. I saw seven or eight hundred troops on the highway, all headed in this direction. They are Redcoats all, most wearing those strange black leather helmets."

"Good Lord!" moaned Bill. "Those must be the Volunteers of Ireland!"

"I do not know who they are, Bill, but they are coming straight at us. And their scouts are not far behind me. They are a half-mile out, maybe less. You have to go back to the Congaree Fort immediately! Warn our officers that the enemy is coming!"

Bill's face clouded with worry. "What about you?"

William shook his head grimly. "Molly is exhausted. She has been running all-out for over a half-hour. I dare not run her any more. She is a bit old and very precious to me. I will not run her into the ground. Your horse is rested and fresh. You can make it back long before the British arrive. It is only eight miles."

"But, where will you go?" wailed Bill. "You will be captured for sure!"

"Do not worry about me. I know this area well. Molly and I will take to the woods. I will head north. With any luck, I can draw them away from you. But, you must go now! There is no time to waste! Our comrades will be destroyed by this large army!"

Bill nodded. He reached up and shook William's hand. "Good luck, friend."

"I will need it." William smiled grimly. "Now, get going! Your mission is dire."

Bill turned and sprinted up the hill toward the pine thicket. Seconds later, William heard the thundering hooves of his horse as it galloped south through the forest.

William uttered a silent prayer for his companion, then patted Molly's neck. He clucked at her and tugged her reins toward the right. "Let's go, girl. I know you are tired, but we must make our escape."

To the north, there was a long section of rocky ground near the river's edge. Hoping to disguise his trail, William urged Molly onto the rocks. The trusty horse proceeded carefully, choosing each step with precision, and making sure that she did not lose her footing. William kept her on this course for almost forty yards and then turned her slightly to the northwest, into yet another stand of tall pine trees. The ground below was covered with a thick carpet of orange-brown needles. They would hide the horse's tracks well.

William rode for almost an hour at a very slow pace. He listened carefully but heard no one following behind him. He saw no sign of the enemy. He heard no more gunshots. It seemed that he had successfully made his escape. Surely, Bill was well on his way back to the fort. He would, no doubt, deliver the news to General Sumpter. The Patriot army would be saved.

As he rode, William kept an eye out for a place to make camp. It would be dark in a couple of hours. Both he and

Molly needed the rest. He soon discovered a perfect spot near a small creek. The water in the creek was clean and clear. The place was protected by a rock bluff on the north side. There was even a shallow rock overhang in the hillside ... a most unusual formation in this area of South Carolina. He would be able to build his fire close to the overhang and keep warm from the wind.

Quickly, William set up his emergency camp. He removed Molly's saddle, gave her a quick rub-down, and then hobbled her beside the stream. He fed her a small pile of oats. His horse well-tended, he then collected an ample pile of dry fuel for his campfire and broke out his fire-starting kit. Skillfully, he put flint to steel and soon enjoyed a toasty fire. After laying out his blankets, he ate a handful of parched corn and drank some water.

Darkness descended quickly in the deep forest. Since there were no other tasks to perform, William decided to rest. He would sleep for a few hours and then break camp and move northward in the middle of the night. He prayed that no one was after him. Even if they were, they, too, would need to stop for the night and make camp. If he departed several hours before dawn, he could successfully put several miles between himself and any pursuers.

William lay down beside his fire. He turned onto his right side and faced the stones of the bluff, allowing the fire to warm his back. Almost instantly, he descended into the deep, restful sleep of utter exhaustion.

WILLIAM DID NOT KNOW how long he had slept. It could not have been long, because his fire still burned bright. But, what had awakened him? He listened carefully. He heard

Molly pawing at the ground near the creek. Something had disturbed her. Somewhere behind him, he heard a twig snap! Then there was the sound of footsteps!

He immediately flipped over onto his back. His heart sank. Standing over him were two scarlet-coated soldiers. The one nearest to his head displayed an evil grin.

"Hello there, laddie," the fellow declared in a thick Irish voice. "We been a lookin' for you. You gave us quite a chase, indeed. But, there be no need fer ya to be a wakin' up on our account."

The fellow then lifted his musket and plunged the stock downward onto William's face with a vicious blow. William heard an odd crunching sound deep inside his head. Then everything in his world disappeared into blackness.

11

REBEL PRISONER

The Next Morning

The blackness gave way to a dull gray. Slowly, William's unconscious mind crawled back toward the waking world. But, try as he might, he could not convince his eyes to open. His eyelids felt as if they each weighed a thousand pounds. Since his vision refused to cooperate, William focused his attention upon his other senses. He smelled a dank, musty, metallic odor. He felt an odd sensation of movement. He was swaying to and fro and, occasionally, bouncing up and down.

At long last, he coaxed his reluctant eyes to open. He was lying flat on his belly. For a long while he remained silent and still as he attempted to discern where he lay. It took some time for his vision to come into full focus. When it did, the first thing he observed was old, gray wood. Less than a foot away from his face was an upright slab of lumber that resembled some sort of wall. His left cheek rested upon another similar piece of wood. He could feel the irritating splinters scratching against his cold skin. Then, it came to him. He was riding in the bed of a wagon. The violent, jostling motion of the vehicle left little doubt.

"*Someone is taking me somewhere,*" he thought. Suddenly, a fearful notion struck him. "*Where is my horse? Where is Molly?*"

He wanted to lift his head and look around, but the pain was too great. William's forehead throbbed. His last memory was that of a musket stock falling toward his face. No doubt, he had been clubbed on the head. His injury was so severe that his entire face actually ached. He worked the muscles in his cheeks in an attempt to stretch them and somehow diminish the pain, but the effort only intensified it. He instinctively tried to reach upward to touch his wounded forehead, but, strangely, his arms would not move. To make matters worse, his shoulders ached horribly.

As his mind continued to process his predicament, he soon discovered the reason for both the aching in his shoulders and his inability to move his arms. His wrists were bound tightly behind his back. He could feel the rough rope digging into his flesh.

"*Lord help me,*" he mumbled. "*I am a prisoner!*"

William finally lifted his head in an attempt to examine his surroundings. That was no small task, either. The skin of his face and his matted hair were stuck to the floor of the wagon, bound there by a frozen, sticky pool of blood. It was, no doubt, his own blood, which had flowed from the wound on his skull.

Suddenly, William became aware that he was very, very cold. He glanced downward at his shoulders. He saw only his bloodstained linen shirt. Both his overcoat and waistcoat were gone. His heart began to race from worry and fear. He could see his labored breaths condensing in the frigid air in front of his face. It was a bitterly cold day. Surely, his captors did not intend to allow him to freeze to death!

William needed a better view. Perhaps, if he could glimpse the countryside, he might recognize a landmark and then discern his whereabouts. But, in order to see beyond the wagon bed, he needed to roll over onto his back. Unfortunately, a large pile of canvas cloths and several wooden boxes blocked his way. With great effort, he scooted his backside close to the wagon's sideboard. He rocked left and right several times and then, using the momentum of his weight, flopped over onto his back. Temporarily exhausted by the strenuous effort, he lay still for a moment and gazed upward at the sky. It was a deep, brilliant, cloudless blue. It did not, at all, resemble the overcast gray sky that he last remembered. Clearly, a considerable amount of time had passed while he was unconscious.

"*How long have I been asleep?*" he wondered. "*One day, or perhaps two?*"

William needed answers. But, in order to find answers, he had to examine his surroundings. He braced himself with his elbows and, with great effort, sat upright. He looked all around. One man was driving the wagon in which he was being held captive. Four Redcoat cavalrymen rode in escort, two in the front and two to the rear. There was no one else in view. The countryside was familiar, indeed. He knew that he was still somewhere west of Camden.

"Watch your back, driver!" warned one of the soldiers riding behind the wagon. "The little devil is awake and stirring about."

The fellow driving the wagon turned slightly to have a quick look at William. He was an older chap, likely in his sixties. His clothes appeared a bit old and shabby, but they were clean and tidy. He wore a gray heavy wool overcoat and an indigo blue wool neck sock. On his head he sported a brown knitted wool cap that was pulled down tightly over his ears.

"Good afternoon, lad," the man greeted him. He offered a smile that seemed friendly enough. "I was beginnin' to worry about you a bit. You look quite a sight, to be sure. You have a nasty cut on your head." He grunted. "And you've made quite a mess of my wagon."

"Where am I?" William demanded tersely.

The fellow returned his attention to the road. "Oh, I'd say we are about three, maybe four miles west of Camden Town. We are making pretty good time. We should arrive around dinner."

William shivered. His teeth chattered from the cold. "I seem to have misplaced my coat and weskit. Do you know where they are?"

The man frowned and then shook his head. "You were dressed as you are when they put you in the wagon. I covered you with some of that canvas when they tossed you in, but you seem to have wiggled out of it. Here, let me help."

Holding the reins with his left hand, the driver reached back with his right hand and grabbed a sheet of old, dirty canvas. He nimbly tossed it across William's head and shoulders.

"There you go. See what you can do with that. It should help a bit."

"Do you always bind your prisoners so tightly?" William scolded as he attempted to burrow beneath the canvas covering. "I cannot even feel my hands."

"Oh, you are no prisoner of mine, lad." He nodded toward one of the Redcoat horsemen. "You are *their* prisoner. I have merely been paid for the services of my wagon. It was a good sum in British silver, so I could hardly refuse."

"Then, you are not a Tory sympathizer?"

The fellow chuckled. "Not likely. I am no sympathizer, at all. Like a lot of other backcountry folk, I serve no cause but my own. I suppose you might say that I have chosen to remain neutral in this war. I serve whoever will pay me the most."

William considered his perilous predicament. "Are you taking me to Camden or someplace further?"

"Only to Camden. I am to deliver you to the jail and then hand you over to the authorities there. These four horsemen are your escorts, here to protect my wagon from attack." Again, he looked back at William and then shook his head grimly. He lowered his voice. "But, it does not please me to deliver you there, lad. You are in a bad spot. A bad spot, indeed. I am told that the British commander has declared you a spy. Do you know what that means?"

William nodded sullenly. "Likely, I will be hanged."

"Aye. And they will leave you danglin' in the tree to rot. You are to be made an example, I fear."

William's mind raced. What could be done? How could he avoid this deadly calamity? Suddenly, the idea came to him. If this fellow was, indeed, partial only to himself and the making of money, he could likely be enticed to deliver a message. Surely, the promise of a payment would be enough to secure his service. But, William knew that he must approach the subject carefully and with caution. He did not want to make matters worse.

"What is your name, sir?" William inquired.

"I am Thaddeus Tolbert of Cedar Creek."

"It is a pleasure to meet you, despite these circumstances. My name is William Newman. My father is Will Newman of Jackson's Creek. Do you know of him?"

The man's head spun around quickly. "Will Newman, you say? He is a known Loyalist, is he not?"

William nodded. "He is."

"But you, his son, serve amongst the rebels?" The man seemed genuinely confused.

William inhaled deeply. "Let us just say that my father and I share differing convictions. Does that surprise you?"

The man shrugged. "I reckon not. You are not alone. I know of many families torn asunder by this ridiculous war."

"No talking!" yelled one of the Redcoats. "Sit quietly, boy, or I will place a gag on you!"

William scooted forward in the wagon bed, inching closer to the driver. He whispered very softly, careful to avoid the attention of the soldiers. "So then, let me understand. You are not sworn or loyal to either side in this conflict?"

The driver lowered his voice as well. "No, I am not. As I said, I serve whoever pays me well." He paused. "Is something on your mind, lad?"

William moved forward until he was almost touching the driver. "Would you consider delivering a message to my father for me? He is a man of means and would reimburse you for your trouble."

The man became quite rigid and still. He remained silent for a while. Clearly, he was considering the offer. The promise of a payment or reward was enticing, indeed.

"Please, Mr. Tolbert," William begged. "You are my only hope."

"Jackson's Creek is several miles out of the way for me. 'Twould be much trouble and cost me much in time."

"My father will pay you well, I promise."

The man leaned back in his seat, bringing himself a little closer to William. "I cannot deliver a written message for you, laddie. I will not risk being arrested for treason to the Crown. If I were caught, I would go to the gallows, as well."

"My hands are bound. I couldn't write a message if I wanted to. I simply ask that you go to my father's home and inform him that I have been captured. Tell him that I am being held at the Camden jail. Tell him that I face the gallows. Will you do this for me? Father will make it worth your time, I promise you."

The man leaned forward and rested his elbows on his knees. He said nothing for a long while. Then, the wagon rounded a bend and the rooftops of Camden came into view. William was becoming frantic. He was only minutes away from prison. Soon, it would be too late. The driver was his only chance to get a message to his father.

"Please, sir," William hissed. "My life is in your hands."

As the wagon passed the faded sign that welcomed people to Camden, the driver turned his head and stared into William's eyes. He mumbled, "I do not think it will make any difference for you, boy ... but I'll deliver your message."

"Thank you, Mr. Tolbert," William whispered. "Thank you so much!"

"I said no talking!" the soldiers barked again. "Do not make me say it again, or I will run you through!"

The dragoon brought his horse closer, whipped out his sword, and then slapped the flat of the blade across William's back. The hard steel stung his frozen flesh. William yelped in pain.

"Back away from the driver! Now!"

William pushed himself back a couple of feet. Though his body was freezing cold and his back was burning with pain, his heart was warm on the inside. Soon, his father would know his whereabouts. There was a chance, albeit a small one, that something might be done. There was still hope.

The wagon jostled through the rough, rutted streets of the town. William knew Camden well and realized that they would soon arrive at the jail. He almost welcomed it. At least, inside the stone walls of the jail, there would be some respite from the bitter winter cold. There might even be a blanket and fire.

"Whoa, girls!" called the driver, pulling on the reins.

The wagon eased to a stop. The driver climbed down and then walked to the rear of the wagon. He removed the back board and then extended his hand to assist William. The freezing, bound boy struggled onto his knees, anxious to get indoors. Slowly, and with the driver's assistance, he climbed down from the wagon. Instantly, his heart fell in his chest when he heard a horrifyingly familiar voice.

"Well, well now. Look who we have here. I recognize you, even with all that bloody mess all over your face. It is none other than William Newman, the traitor of Jackson's Creek!"

Standing on the stone steps was the Camden jailer. He was the man who had beaten William all those months ago and who had taken such pleasure in his mistreatment. His grotesquely evil face displayed a devilish, hungry grin.

The commander of the British guard handed the jailer a document. "I hereby convey this rebel spy into your charge. You will do unto him as the law demands."

"Thank you, Lieutenant," the jailer answered. He took the document, unfolded it, and read its contents.

"Now, isn't this dandy? It is exactly as I claimed before. You *are* a rebel spy, captured in the field and under arms against the King. Didn't I tell you that you would be back in my care, and soon? Oh, 'twill not be long now. Soon, my boy, you will dangle from the end of my rope. And I have a special one chosen just for you."

He reached out and grabbed William roughly by the arm. He gave the lad a harsh jerk. The pain in William's stiff shoulder caused him to cry out.

"That's it, lad! That's the sound that I like to hear. 'Tis sweet music to my ears. And to think that we are just getting started. It just makes my heart all warm and happy. Now, come on inside, you little turncoat. We have much re-acquainting to do. I have your old room all ready and waiting for you."

One Week Later
March 1, 1781

WILLIAM DID NOT KNOW what day it was. He had no notion as to how long he had been kept in the jail. There was neither day nor night for him. His life was nothing but an endless cycle of interrogation, beatings, torture, and pain. He longed for it all to end.

Still, despite all that the jailer and the British authorities had inflicted upon him, William did not confess to any crime. He never revealed anything about his fellow soldiers or the military company in which he served. Indeed, he did not even admit the fact that he was a soldier in the American army. He kept silent and, in a very manly display of courage, remained steadfast in the face of the injustices heaped upon him.

His stubborn silence had frustrated his captors. They needed nothing short of a confession. He had heard one of his guards whisper that fact to another of his coworkers in the jail. The Camden magistrate, the same fellow who had presided over William's previous case, had already ruled thusly. There was no evidence that verified William Newman was a spy. He carried no documents nor any equipment of a military nature. Ultimately, they had no proof against him. Therefore, if he was to be convicted and hanged, he *had* to confess.

So, the mistreatment continued. William had just weathered another beating at the hands of the angry, frustrated jailer. How many such beatings had he already endured? Was it seven, or perhaps eight? He lost count. Still reeling from the pain, he lay huddled against the wall of his damp, cold cell. He was so very cold that his entire body was numb. He had no clothing or blankets to protect him. He was naked except for a tattered pair of threadbare linen breeches. His captors had taken away the remainder of his clothing, leaving him to suffer from exposure in the midst of the winter cold.

The gnawing pain deep inside his belly was almost as unbearable as the pain in his members. William was starving. He had not eaten a morsel since his arrival. And, to make matters worse, he was afflicted with a severe sickness. His body shuddered, not only from the cold, but from a raging fever. He had received no medical attention since his arrival. The bleeding wound on his head was swollen and festered. The oozing cut gave off such a horrid odor that it made him gag.

Young William Newman was clinging to life by a narrow, fragile thread. He had lost all hope. In the end, he prayed for death. There was nothing else for him. Constantly, he prayed that this would be the day that he would finally go to the gallows. At least, then, he would no longer be cold, and the pain that ravaged his broken body would stop.

William was just beginning to drift off into a troubled sleep when he heard keys rattling in the lock. Instantly, his heart filled with dread. Why would they be coming after him again so soon? Ordinarily, they waited many hours in between beatings. Or, had it, perhaps, been hours already? Had he simply lost his sense of time in this ghastly, unthinkable, unbearable place?

Suddenly, the room filled with dancing, yellow-orange candlelight. William attempted to roll over onto his back so that he might look toward the door, but his frozen muscles refused to budge. He merely lay still and waited for whatever was to come.

A strangely familiar voice exclaimed, "Good Lord! Just look at the poor boy!"

Moments later, strong hands gripped William and then gently rolled him over onto his back. The light emitting from candle lanterns blinded him. He could not see who was there. An icy-cold hand touched his face and neck.

"This lad is burning with fever! And his face has been beaten beyond recognition! What have you been doing to him?"

"I did what was expected of me, Magistrate," barked the jailer. "This man is a traitor to the Crown. He deserves whatever he gets."

William's eyes had become more adjusted to the bright light. He recognized the magistrate from his previous hearing. The government official sounded livid.

"As I told you before, Mr. Tuttle, I found no evidence against him. Only a confession would be sufficient to punish him. But, I did not intend for that to be a license for you to beat one out of him." He exhaled in disgust. "When the

Reverend Adams informed me of what he saw going on in this jail, I refused to believe him. But now I see this! Good God, man! It is barbaric!"

"I am only doing my duty according to the law, sir!" retorted the jailer.

"Well, your duty shall no longer include responsibility over this boy. And if I have my way, you will have no more authority over this jail, either!" He called past the jailer to two men who were standing outside in the hallway. "You two! Guards! Get in here and bring this boy out at once! I want him delivered to the hospital with haste. Fetch blankets and broth." He glared at the jailer. "I pray, for your sake, that this boy lives. For, if he does not, you may be the one who will go to the gallows!"

The two guards standing in the hallway entered. They quickly lifted William from the floor. He lost consciousness as they carried him out the door of the cell.

WILLIAM'S EYES FLUTTERED OPEN. He was warm. It was such a wonderful, comforting feeling. As his vision came into focus, the smiling face that greeted him caused his heart to leap with joy.

"Papa!" he moaned in a dry, parched voice. He could barely make a sound. "How can you be here?"

Will Newman, his eyes filling with tears, caressed his son's hand. "The wagoner, Mr. Tolbert, brought me your message. He is the reason I found you." He gently lifted his son's head as he offered him a cup of water. "Here, Son. Drink this. It will help your throat."

William gratefully received the drink. He swallowed

slowly, allowing the cool fluid to trickle down his scorched throat.

He glanced around the room where he lay. It was an unfamiliar place. "Where am I?" His voice sounded stronger. "This is certainly not the jail."

"You are in the hospital. Son, you have been very ill."

William was confused. "This does not look like the Camden hospital." As he scanned the room, he frowned. The place was dingy, dirty, and most unpleasant. "Indeed, it does not look like much of a hospital at all." He pulled his worn, stained bedcovers upward to cover his nose. "The stench is almost as bad as that inside the jail."

"This is a military-run hospital, set up for rebel soldiers and prisoners." He frowned. "You are still a prisoner, William. That has not changed. However, the authorities no longer regard you as a spy. You will remain here until you are well enough to travel, and then you will be transported to Charlestown."

"When?"

"Three days hence, I'm told," his father responded grimly.

"They will take me to a prison ship?"

Will's chin dropped sullenly to his chest. His lip quivered slightly. "Yes."

"Well, Father, it cannot be any worse than the Camden jail. And it is certainly better than the gallows." He forced himself to smile as he patted his father's arm reassuringly. "Everything will be all right. You will see." Again, he looked around the room. "How long have I been here in this hospital?"

"Three weeks," Will responded, frowning.

"Three weeks?" exploded William. "How? Have I truly been asleep that long?"

His father nodded. "You awakened only a handful of times. But, with your horrible fever, you were not yourself. I doubt that you would remember."

William closed his eyes, thinking. "I vaguely remember being removed from my cell. The old magistrate was there, I recall. I remember how I thought it odd to see him there in the jail."

Will nodded. "He was there. I begged him to go and see you. I arrived in Camden two days after you got here. I tried to gain your release, but my efforts were fruitless. No one, not even the magistrate, would listen or speak with me. I finally convinced a local minister, the Reverend Amos Adams, to visit inside the jail and check on you. When he saw you through the door, he was so disturbed that he made a personal report to the magistrate. That is what led to the official visit and, ultimately, to your being brought out of the prison to the hospital."

"Was I in a bad way?"

"A bad way?" exclaimed his father, chuckling sarcastically. "Son, you were at the very edge of death! You had a raging fever. You had lost almost twenty pounds. Your toes were almost black from the cold. And that wound on your head was festered. You would have died, for certain, if you had remained in that jail. 'Tis no small wonder that you survived, even here in the hospital. You would have perished, were it not for your tireless, dedicated caregiver."

William was perplexed. "Caregiver? Whatever do you mean, Father?"

Suddenly, a door opened on the far side of the room. Then came a pattering of light footsteps upon the rough wooden floor of the ward. A soft, sweet voice from behind Will Newman exclaimed, "Is he awake?" There was a gasp of joy. "Oh! Praise be! He *is* awake!"

William then caught a glimpse the most beautiful face that he had ever in his life seen. She was every bit an angel. Her lovely, perfect cheeks flushed red with joy and excitement. It was his beloved, Mary Austin.

"Mary! Oh, Mary ... what on earth are you doing here?" blurted William.

Will Newman beamed with pleasure and pride. "She has been helping me care for you, Son. She has been utterly tireless in her efforts. Surely, she is the one who has kept you alive all these days."

"But ... but ... I do not understand," William stammered. "When we last spoke, you made it absolutely clear that we were through. You told me that you could not be wed to a turncoat." He appeared on the verge of tears. "I assumed that you did not love me anymore."

Mary stared adoringly at William. "Oh, William, surely, after all these years, you must know and understand my moods. I was upset and confused. I said some things out of emotion that I have come to regret. After you departed to join in the war, it was as if a portion of my heart left with you. Truly, I am sorry for those cruel things that I said. I'm sorry that I pushed you away. I hope that you can forgive me. I have given my heart to you, no matter your politics."

William's face glowed with joy. "You make me so happy, Mary. But, how did you ever convince your father to allow you to come here ... to a rebel prison hospital?"

Mary plopped down on the edge of his bed. "I did not seek my father's permission, as I did not need it. I merely informed him that my future husband lay at death's door, and that I must go and attend him." She shrugged. "He is angry with me, of course. But, that is nothing new. Lately, he has grown into an unhappy, curmudgeonly old fellow. Likely, he will not speak to me for a long while. But, I do not care. Likewise, I care not for his politics, or his wars, or even King George, for that matter."

"Shh!" hissed William's father. "Be careful, girl. Remember where you are!"

"Oh, I don't care! What could they possibly do to me?" She reached out and took William's hand. She stared deeply and lovingly into his eyes. "I only care for you, William Newman."

William smiled warmly. "And I for you, Mary Austin."

She leaned in close to him. "Now, I need you to eat and rest and heal. Soon you will need all your strength."

William frowned. "I know. They are sending me to the prison ship in three days."

She leaned close to him and placed her lips against his ear. She whispered softly, "You will never see a prison ship. Your brother knows you are here. Colonel Winn knows, as well. Take heart, my love. They are coming to rescue you!"

12

RESCUE!

It was well after midnight. A respectable woman should not be out in the streets at such a late hour. But, on this particular night, Mary Austin was not worried about such things as good manners and respectabilty. Instead, she was acting as a rebel and a traitor to the Crown. Mary Austin was a Patriot spy! She carried valuable information for the American militia ... information that would help her beloved, William Newman, to go free.

Mary moved slowly and stealthily through the deserted streets of Camden. At last, she reached the alleyway that would take her to the place where she was to meet her rebel contact. She crept past the blacksmith's shop, remaining close against the building and concealing herself in the shadows. When she reached the corner just beyond, she paused and then nervously scanned the street behind her. She saw no one. Turning left into the narrow alley, she darted quickly toward the city cemetery. Someone was supposed to be waiting to meet her there.

It was a cloudless night and there was a full moon. The

huge, glowing nighttime orb bathed the town with a gleam of silver-blue. Shadows appeared everywhere. Mary's imagination was running wild. She was terrified. He fear caused her to run faster. Soon, she reached the cemetery gates. She sprinted through the opening and then quickly concealed herself behind a stone wall. She waited, listened, and wondered. Her mind reeled with questions. *Was her contact coming? Was she too early? Had the British tricked her and laid a trap for her?*

Mary jumped, startled, when an unexpected, low voice spoke from the darkness. "Were you followed?"

"No!" she whispered. "No one else is out. The streets are empty. The town is asleep."

A tall, lean figure stepped from behind a large oak. He was clad in buckskin breeches and a dark green wool coat. He had two flintlock pistols tucked inside his belt. He wore a black floppy hat pulled down low over his face.

The man stepped closer, moving out of the shadows, and then declared, "It is good to see you, Mary. It has been a long time."

Mary recognized the voice immediately. It was Austin Newman, William's older brother. She tumbled into his arms and hugged him tightly.

"Oh, Austin! I am so glad to see you!"

"Come," Austin urged. "Let us hide over there in that thicket amongst the trees."

Tugging her gently by the arm, Austin led Mary into the shadows of several squatty oaks. As it was winter, there were no leaves on the trees. But, the thick trunks made the thicket a dark, shadowy place. The thicket was well away from the gate and the road, and offered a good place of concealment. Quickly, silently, they knelt together beneath one of the trees.

"What have you learned?" Austin asked immediately, wasting no time. "How is William to be transported to Charlestown? By river or by road?"

"The Wateree River," Mary answered succinctly.

"When? How many men?"

"They depart by flatboat at dawn on the day after tomorrow. There will be ten to twelve prisoners in the group. There will be the boatsman, of course, and no more than four or five guards." She grinned in the darkness. "I heard two of the Tory guards discussing it all over breakfast at the tavern this morning. They paid no attention to me at all."

Austin nodded and patted her on the hand. "Good job. That is excellent information, Mary. We were hoping they would go downriver. There are plenty of places on the Wateree where we can lay an ambush."

"But, what if William is harmed during your attack?" Mary's voice cracked with emotion.

"Do not worry about that. My little brother will suffer no harm. I promise you."

"Oh, thank you, Austin!" She hugged him again.

"I must go now, Mary. There is much to do. You should return to your lodging by a different route. Be careful and stay in the shadows of the buildings. Understand?"

"Yes. I will be very careful. But, what shall I tell William?"

"Just tell him that we are coming for him during his little boat ride. And tell him that, if and when any shooting starts, he must get down and stay low."

"Please watch out for him, Austin," Mary begged.

"Do not worry, Mary. I will rescue your little turncoat." He grinned. His white teeth glowed in the moonlight. "I will see you again very soon."

Austin kissed her affectionately on the forehead and

then rose to his feet. He was gone in an instant, melting silently into the thick brush that surrounded the cemetery.

Two Days Later

IT WAS EARLY AFTERNOON. William sat with ten other prisoners in the floor of the slowly-moving flatboat. The men were shackled together at the ankles by an elaborate system of interlocking iron chains. It was a pleasantly mild and sunny winter day. The men were actually enjoying being out in the warm sunshine. For some, it had been many days since they had been outdoors. Indeed, several of the Patriot prisoners had been confined inside their lightless basement jail cells for many weeks.

There were four armed Tory militiamen assigned to the boat, each seated on wooden boxes at the four corners. Though tasked with keeping watch and guarding the prisoners, none of the men seemed overly concerned with their duties. Only one guard was actually holding his musket. One of the men was reclining against the rail and reading a pamphlet. Another was dangling a fishing line from the rear of the boat, hoping to snag a stray fish. The fourth guard was actually asleep, his head resting precariously on the side rail of the boat.

The only man amongst the Tories who remained focused and vigilant was Tuttle, the former jailer. Several days prior, he had been removed from his post at the Camden jail by the magistrate. But, after calling in some personal favors with other area officials, he had somehow managed to gain command of this guard detail. He was tasked with delivering the prisoners to Charlestown. Tuttle sat on a chair on the small upper-deck next to the talkative boatsman. He was armed with a sword and two pistols. Though the boatsman tirelessly attempted to engage him in conversation, Tuttle spoke little. He had no interest in socializing. Instead, he maintained careful watch over the prisoners in his charge.

Once, around mid-morning, William had made the mistake of making eye contact with the vile, vengeful man. Tuttle glared at William with a hate-filled gaze. Then, his lips curled into an evil grin as he reached down and tapped on the stock of one of his pistols with his forefinger. The man's look and threatening gesture sent a shiver down William's spine. William determined not to look at him again.

William was actually perplexed by Tuttle's presence on the boat. He was uncertain as to why the man had worked so hard to receive command of this prisoner transport detail. The obvious reason seemed to be that he was attempting to earn his way back into his old job at the jail. One of William's fellow prisoners suggested that, since his reputation was ruined in Camden, he was merely earning free passage downriver to Charlestown. A ruined man could make a fresh start in a new place, especially a large city.

But William had other ideas. He suspected that Tuttle had more sinister intentions. The former jailer was a bitter, angry, vengeful man. He held a deep grudge toward William Newman. Surely, he blamed the lad for the loss of his job and the status that he had enjoyed in Loyalist Camden. William feared that he was looking for the opportunity to take his revenge.

William attempted to dismiss the unpleasant thoughts of Tuttle from his mind. Instead, he focused upon the pleasant, warm weather and sunshine that warmed his body. He also fixed his mind upon the rescue that was sure to come. And he prayed that it might come soon.

The flatboat was approaching yet another sharp, narrow bend in the river. The Wateree was filled with such turns. It was a lazy, snake-like waterway that wound its way back and forth in a general southward direction toward the Congaree. The boatsman, obviously an experienced man on the rudder and familiar with the wandering river, had guided his craft around several similar turns with ease. He steered the craft toward the western bank, careful to avoid a shallow sandbar on the eastern side. He then allowed the current to take the craft. Soon, he cut back toward the left and almost effortlessly guided the boat around the bend.

Suddenly, after clearing the bend in the river, the flat-boat gave a mighty lurch forward. The bow dipped down slightly as the boat came to a complete and violent stop. All of the guards were tossed from their makeshift seats. The sleeping guard on the starboard bow actually flipped over the railing and landed in the cold, muddy water with a loud splash. The prisoners, all chained together and sitting on the floor of the boat, fared somewhat better. Tuttle was thrown forward from his chair, tumbling off of the upper deck and landing in the bottom of the boat with a resounding thud. Several of the prisoners chuckled mockingly at his fall.

"What the devil?" growled the boatsman, still clinging to his rudder pole.

The crimson-faced Tuttle jumped to his feet. He gave the nearest prisoner a swift, angry kick with his boot. He pointed forward and shouted at the remaining guard, "Don't just stand there like a moron! Toss that man a line! Get him out of the water!"

The fellow moved quickly to obey his superior. As he

pulled the soaked fellow back onto the boat, the boatsman jumped down from the top deck and began walking forward.

Instinctively, William knew that this was the moment that he had been waiting for. This was the ambush site. Quietly and stealthily, William tapped the leg of the fellow beside him. He whispered, "Rescue. Stay low. Pass the word."

The fellow nodded. Immediately, he turned to his left and conveyed the message to the next man. It took mere seconds to inform all of the prisoners. Silently, hopefully, they all huddled together and hugged close to the bottom deck of the boat.

As William waited for the combat to begin, he scanned the area near him, searching for anything he might utilize as a weapon. There was nothing. With the heavy irons binding his ankles, he could not reach more than three or four feet in any direction. Disappointed, he resolved himself to remain still and wait to be rescued.

"What is blocking us, Jenkins?" demanded Tuttle. "Why have we stopped? Is there a sandbar or a log in the way?"

The captain of the boat leaned forward over the front rail and peered into the water. "No, I do not see any logs. And there are no sandbars out here in the middle of the channel. The water is far too deep." He walked toward the port side. When he reached the corner of the boat, he leaned far over the rail and reached down, probing below the water line. Immediately, he stood upright and spun around. He exclaimed, "There is a rope, less than a foot below the water! Someone has blocked the river!"

At that very moment, one of the guards at the stern gave a frantic shout. "Ambush!" He lifted his musket and aimed it toward the trees on the eastern bank.

The sharp crack of a distant flintlock pierced the silence of the surrounding forest. A puff of gray-white smoke billowed from the nearby trees. The guard immediately dropped his musket, staggered for a moment, and then tumbled sideways over the rail and into the river. There was a loud splash. The poor fellow was dead before he hit the water.

A voice called out from behind the gray shadows of the trees. "The rest of you stay where you are! Lay down your weapons! There is no need for anyone else to die here today."

Colonel Richard Winn stepped out of the tree line on the western side of the river. Austin Newman followed closely behind him. Both men had their weapons aimed at the boat.

"I shall not bow to the demands of lowlife thieves," retorted Tuttle. He thrust his chest forward proudly. "I am Josiah Tuttle, acting on behalf of the King of England. I have been tasked to deliver these prisoners to Charlestown. You, sir, are interfering with the work of the Crown. You have murdered one of the King's soldiers. You shall hang for your treason!"

Colonel Winn spat disgustedly on the ground. "Yours is not the first such threat that I have heard lately, Tuttle. I'm sure that King George and his minions have plenty of reasons to hang a fellow like me."

"Who are you?" demanded Tuttle. "And how do you know my name?"

"You should know who I am, Josiah. We played together as children. I am Richard Winn, colonel and commander of the Fairfield District Militia."

Tuttle's eyes widened. His lips curled into a wicked grin. "Little Dickie Winn. Yes, I remember you. So, now you are a rebel scoundrel. I might have known. It has been many years, indeed. Finally, we meet again."

"Yes, Josiah. Finally, we meet again." He pointed toward the prisoners. "You will surrender your prisoners into my custody. If you do so, I will cut the rope and allow you and your men to keep your boat and proceed downstream in peace."

Tuttle's face flushed an angry red. "And if I do not surrender them?"

"Then, Josiah, you will bear the consequences. No doubt, you will die." His eyes narrowed threateningly. "Do not test me, Josiah. I am hungry, tired, and in a foul mood."

Tuttle grunted sarcastically. "Your words are pretty tall talk for a mere two men."

Austin lifted his fingers to his mouth and unleashed a piercing whistle. Instantly, forty armed soldiers emerged from the trees on both sides of the river. They surrounded the boat. William's heart leapt when he recognized the rifleman standing beside his brother, Austin. It was his father! Will Newman had accompanied the rebel militia!

Tuttle became so angry that he actually trembled. He was accustomed to being the man in power. But now, he was utterly powerless. There was no way that he could resist. It was only he and his three remaining Tory militiamen standing against forty armed attackers.

"Well?" demanded Colonel Winn. "What say you now? Are you ready to comply?"

Frantic, Josiah Tuttle scanned the men along both banks of the river. Suddenly, he recognized the man standing near to Richard Winn. It was Will Newman, the father of his prisoner! He was no longer dressed in the clothing of a gentleman, but there was no mistaking him.

Tuttle was no fool. He instantly discerned that Will

Newman was the cause of this brazen raid upon the King's boat. He was here, with the help of his rebel friends and neighbors, to rescue his son. Immediately, he realized that the lad, William Newman, provided his only possible way out of this situation.

Quick as a flash, Tuttle sprang to his left and grabbed William up off of the floor. He whipped his pistol from his belt and then jammed the muzzle threateningly against William's right temple.

"I know now what this foolishness is all about," sneered Tuttle. He glared hatefully at Will. "You are here to fetch your little traitor back home to his mama." He pulled back the flintlock, placing the gun on full cock. If he pulled the trigger, William would certainly die. "Well, I shall not let you have him! You may take this boat, but you will never get this boy!"

"Put the gun down, Josiah!" barked Colonel Winn. "As I said before, there is no need for more violence. Just release the prisoners and be on your way."

"I will not!" growled Tuttle. "You shall not have them! None of them!" He violently jabbed the steel barrel against William's head. "Especially this one."

William was becoming frustrated. Despite the gun to his head, he shouted angrily, "Would someone please shoot this scoundrel? Put him down like the Tory dog that he is!"

"Shut your filthy rebel mouth!" Tuttle barked. He swung the pistol and struck William violently across the back of his head.

William winced in pain. He stumbled forward, but remained standing because of Tuttle's firm grasp upon his arm. He shook his head to dispel the pain and clear his vision. He glanced helplessly at his father and brother. Both men were mad with worry. William could see a tear of anguish creeping down his father's cheek.

For sure, William was in a tight spot. He suddenly realized that if he was going to make it off of the boat alive, *he* would have to take action. Quickly, he devised a plan. If he could only knock Tuttle off-balance, even for just a moment, then perhaps one of the militiamen could get off a quick shot. It was his only hope. But how could he communicate his plan?

William soon locked eyes with his father. Knowing that he had Will's attention, he quickly cut his eyes to the right, in the direction of the pistol that was against his head. Then, he gave his right shoulder a slight wiggle. The movement was barely visible. Will, confused, narrowed his eyes and cocked his head in concentration. He knew that his son was trying to send him a message, but he could not figure out what it was.

Again, William shifted his eyes toward Tuttle and his gun. Then, very slowly, he brought his left hand in front of his body with his thumb up and forefinger pointing in Tuttle's direction, forming the universal symbol of a gun. He narrowed his eyes and gave his pretend gun a subtle jerk.

Instantly, Will knew that his son was about to make a move. He nodded at William and then slowly raised his rifle and took careful aim. Austin, though he did not know what was going on, reacted to his father's action. He also lifted his rifle and took aim at Tuttle.

Josiah Tuttle saw their movements. He instantly stepped behind William, taking partial cover behind the boy.

"No funny business, Newman!" Tuttle growled. "I see you aiming that gun at me. If you shoot me, you will shoot your boy, as well."

Again, William made the sign of the gun with his hand.

He nodded slightly to his father and brother. Neither of them acknowledged him. They were too focused upon the aim of their rifles. William could only hope that they understood him.

William closed his eyes and took a deep breath. He prayed that he had communicated his message clearly and that his father and brother knew what to do. Slowly, he lowered his left hand back to his side.

Tuttle grinned his customary evil grin. "Well, what's it going to be, Newman? You can either cut that rope and let me pass, or your son dies ... right here, right now."

William subtly opened his left hand, exposing all five of his fingers. Then, one at a time he folded each finger in a silent countdown. 5 ... 4 ... 3 ... 2 ... 1 ...

When his last finger folded and only a fist remained, William thrust his right shoulder up and back, knocking the pistol upward. Lunging backward, he propelled himself with his feet. He violently slammed his body into Tuttle's. The Tory unleashed a profane, angry scream as he lost his balance. Instinctively, he pulled the trigger on his pistol. But, William's head was already far behind the barrel. The shot went high. Still, the loud report was deafening and the blast of the pistol's gunpowder scorched William's face and neck. Completely off-balance, William continued to tumble backward.

As he fell, William heard the sharp crack of two flintlock rifles. The shots were almost simultaneous. Then, just as William landed hard on the deck of the boat, two bullets struck Josiah Tuttle square in the chest. The man slumped down slowly to his knees and then fell face-forward onto the deck. He lay motionless next to William. The horrible, evil man was dead. William was saved. Near the tree line, a cloud of gray-white gunpowder smoke filled the air around Will and Austin Newman.

Will lowered his gun and immediately sprinted to the water's edge. He cried out, "William! Son! Are you all right?"

His ears still ringing from the pistol shot, William slowly rose to his knees. He peered over the top rail and then gave his father a quick smile and wave. His face was black from powder burns, but he was otherwise uninjured. He pried the empty pistol from Tuttle's lifeless hand and then stood. The three remaining Tory guards remained as still as statues. Their mouths hung wide open in dismay.

"What about it, boys?" challenged Colonel Winn. "Do you surrender, or do you intend to fight?"

The three men glanced at one another and then slowly lowered their muskets and dropped them on the deck. All three raised their hands high in the air.

The boatsman then raised his hands as well. He declared, "I reckon my boat is yours, Colonel."

THE NEWMAN MEN embraced on the riverbank. It was a joy-filled family reunion. Will Newman wept as he held both of his brave sons in his arms.

"I simply cannot believe that you are here, Father," William declared, pulling away from his father's embrace. "But, what will you do now? You have taken the life of one of the King's officials. You are a criminal now."

Austin patted his father on his shoulder. "You only did what you had to do, Father. We both did. We had to save our William."

William was still worried. "But, what will you do when you return home, Father? Surely, you will now be counted amongst us rebels. You have joined in with Colonel Winn and the rebel militia. No doubt, the people of Jackson's Creek will find this out before you even get back home. Your reputation as a Loyalist is ruined."

Will shrugged. "I suppose it is. I reckon I have followed both of my sons into treason." He grinned. "But, without doubt, you boys are both worth it."

Colonel Winn interrupted their reunion. "Corporal Newman, I have an important assignment for you."

Austin snapped to attention. "Yes, sir!"

"I want you to escort your father and brother home to Jackson's Creek. You and William are hereby placed on two weeks leave. After that time, you will both return to the regiment. Understood?"

"Yes, sir. We will be back in camp in two weeks."

"Excellent." The colonel nodded to Will. "You have raised some fine sons, Will Newman. It is because of brave boys such as these that we are going to win this war and have ourselves a new nation."

Will smiled. "I quite agree, Richard."

The colonel shook Will's hand. As he turned to walk away, he tipped his hat to young William. "You did good work today, Private Newman. But, your work is not done. We have a war to win." He gave a quick wink. "I'll see you in two weeks, little turncoat."

EPILOGUE

December 14, 1782
Evacuation Day
Charlestown, South Carolina

Finally, the war was over. America had won its independence from Great Britain. It was a glorious victory for the Patriots. It was a costly loss for the British and their Tory allies.

It was Evacuation Day in South Carolina. Over 10,000 British and Hessian troops, along with thousands of Loyalist civilians, were being forcibly removed from the state. Throngs of mandatory evacuees were being escorted by armed troops to over one hundred and thirty British ships in Charlestown harbor. Those ships would take them away from the United States of America.

Most of the Loyalists had already lost their lands and properties. All over the state, regional militia officers had compiled lists of men who had taken up arms against the United States. If those men had not sworn their oaths to South Carolina and to the Congress in a timely manner, they were automatically placed on the removal list for mandatory evacuation.

Sadly, Bartholomew Austin, his sons, and all of the members of their families were on that list.

The Austins stood near the Charlestown docks and awaited the calling of their names. Soon, they would leave. Mary Austin Newman, freshly married to young William, clung to her mother and wept. The Newmans waited with them, determined to support their friends right up until the bitter end.

"Surely, Bat, there must be something we can do!" Will Newman blurted, exasperated. "This is simply wrong. You only took up arms once, and that was back in 1775."

Bat shook his head. Clearly, he was defeated. "My sons fought for King George throughout the entire war. No, my old friend. It is over. I have exhausted every possible appeal, right up to the acting governor. I am afraid that this is to be our last day in America."

"But, you have never lived anywhere else!" Will protested. "Your father and grandfather were born here. America is your home!"

Bat patted his friend on the shoulder. "Do not worry about us, Will. We shall be just fine. We are better off than most of the other folk getting on these ships today. We still have some money and our clothing."

"But, where will you go?" moaned Lizzy.

Bat held his head high and proud. "I heard that our ship is bound for Newfoundland. We shall make a life there, I suppose."

"That is in Canada," Austin declared. There was a glimmer of hope in his voice. "It is not so far. You can get back here from Canada. After things calm down in a few years, you *must* make your way southward again. We will make a place for you."

Bat shrugged sadly. "Perhaps. We shall see."

A Continental Army Major approached with a paper in hand. He called out, "Austin! Bartholomew Austin!"

Bat raised his hand. "I am Bartholomew Austin."

"Mr. Austin, I see that we have listed here eight souls in your family under orders of evacuation."

"No, sir. There are only seven."

"Please explain," demanded the major impatiently.

"My daughter, Mary, has married William Newman. He was a soldier in the rebel ... I mean ... the American militia. She is now bound to her husband."

"I see," the Major remarked skeptically. "Is the girl here with you today?"

"She is." Bat gently pulled Mary away from her mother and placed her hand in William's. "Show him the document, William."

Young William reached into the interior pocket of his linen coat and produced a parchment stamped by the county clerk in Camden Town. It was his and Mary's marriage license, attested by the regional commissioner.

"Very well then," the major declared, handing the paper back to William. "Mrs. Austin will, of course, remain here with her lawful husband. But, the rest of you must follow me now. By act of Congress and the South Carolina legislature, you will depart these shores, never to return. If you will accompany me, please." He motioned his hand toward an awaiting boat.

Will Newman and Bat Austin, his lifelong friend, shook hands and then hugged. Mary once again clung to her mother and wept even more loudly than before. William had to wrestle her from her mother's embrace. Mary turned and immediately buried her face in his chest. She could not bear to watch them go. She wept openly, her heart broken by the forced separation.

Bat and his sons immediately picked up the family's bags and then proceeded toward the gangplank that led up onto the awaiting ship. Rachel Austin walked sullenly behind her husband. Their sons, daughters-in-law, and grandchildren followed. They slowly marched up the dancing, bowing plank and then disappeared past the railing onto the deck of the ship. They did not look back.

The Newmans waited as the ship was prepared for sailing. They scanned the decks constantly, hoping to catch one last glimpse of their friends. They wanted to wave to them one last time. But, sadly, the Austin family never came up onto the deck.

Soon, the dock hands released the ropes. Men with long poles pushed the ship out into the current of the river. The huge vessel slowly began to pull away. It sailed across the harbor at a frustratingly slow pace. After almost a half-hour, the boat rounded the tip of James Island and then disappeared completely from view.

"Will we ever see our friends again?" Lizzy mused mournfully.

"I hope so," declared Will. "But, for now, we must see to our own care. Let us return to the tavern and have supper. We will retire early tonight. We have a very long journey upriver tomorrow, and we have much work to do when we get back home. I am certain that Austin is anxious to see us return."

Young William kissed his lovely wife softly on the cheek. "Come, Mary Newman. Let us go and make for ourselves a new home in the backcountry. Are you ready?"

Mary lifted her eyes to her husband. Though heartbroken, she smiled. "I am ready, William. You are my only family now."

Lizzy Newman placed her hand gently on Mary's shoulder. "No, my dear. We are *all* your family. Forever."

Mary wiped her tears with her handkerchief. She smiled at Lizzy and nodded. "I am ready. Let's go home."

The members of the Newman family, Patriots of Fairfield District in South Carolina, turned and trudged slowly away from the waterfront. Mary never saw her family again.

REVOLUTIONARY WAR / COLONIAL GLOSSARY

Barracks – A form of housing or dormitory for soldiers. Their primary function was for sleeping. Often dozens of men were housed in these large buildings.

Bayonet – The sharp knife-like instrument that connects to the end of a military musket. It was used most often in hand-to-hand fighting.

Bedchamber – The common 18th century word for bedroom.

Blockhouse – The corner structure that was usually included into the structure of the walls of a fort.

Breeches – These were the pants of the colonial period. They were secured with buttons and baggy in the seat. The pants reached just below the knee. Men typically wore long socks that covered their lower leg and extended up over the knee.

Brown Bess Musket – This is the name given to the British Army's military musket. They were mass-produced, smooth-barreled flintlock weapons that fired a .75 caliber (¾ inch) round lead ball.

Bullet / Ball / Musket Ball – The round lead balls fired from 18th century weapons.

Bullet Mold – Sized steel molds used to make rifle and musket projectiles. Melted lead was poured into these molds and allowed to cool, thus producing balls perfectly sized for weapons of the period.

Cannon – The artillery of Revolutionary War. These giant guns loaded through the muzzle and fired either large steel balls or clusters of steel or lead known as **grapeshot**.

Canteen – A receptacle used by soldiers to carry their personal supply of water.

Cartridge – These were pre-rolled ammunition packs for muskets. Made from paper, each cartridge resembled a stubby cigar, and contained the proper amount of gunpowder and a single lead projectile. Soldiers tore the cartridges open with their teeth, poured the gunpowder down the barrel of their weapon, and then rammed the paper and musket ball down the barrel.

Cease-Fire – A temporary stoppage of fighting, usually giving officers of opposing armies the opportunity to talk to one another under parley.

Chamber Pot – A porcelain or wooden pot, with lid, that was usually concealed beneath one's bed. During the night, people would relieve themselves (use the bathroom) in this pot to avoid going outside to an outdoor toilet or privy. In a hospital, patients were often provided with chamber pots, since many were unable to walk outside to relieve themselves. Obviously, chamber pots had to be emptied and washed each morning.

Charleville Musket – A French army musket that was common during the period of the American Revolution. It was a smooth-barreled flintlock weapon that fired a .69 caliber round lead ball.

Compatriots – Soldiers who fight alongside one another.

Continental Army – Soldiers in the federal army of the United States as authorized by the Continental Congress.

Crown – The shortened form of "**British Crown.**" It was a reference to the form of British government, which was a kingdom. The king or queen was the wearer of the "crown."

Dragoons – A special type of soldier in the British army. They were "mounted infantry" who could either fight on horseback or on foot.

Earthworks – Piles of dirt, rock, and wood used as a barricade to protect soldiers from enemy gunfire. Soldiers often constructed these around their forts or around places that they were attacking.

Flatboat – A rectangular, flat-bottomed boat used to transport cargo and passengers in inland rivers and waterways. Such boats were specifically designed for and especially useful in shallow waters.

Flintlock – The type of weapons, loaded through the muzzle, used during the American Revolution.

Flux – Also known as "camp fever" or "ship's fever," the flux was a debilitating sickness of diarrhea, often accompanied by intestinal bleeding. It was a deadly disease, and was quite debilitating for an army or for sailors on board a ship. Through modern medicine, we now know the disease as dysentery. It was and is today transmitted through fecal contamination of water supplies.

Fowling Gun / Fowler – A multi-use smoothbore flintlock weapon. Using small pellets of bird shot, a hunter could use the weapon for hunting birds (fowling) or small game such as rabbits or squirrels. For large game, such as deer, elk, or bear, the weapon would also fire a lead round ball (bullet). Such a gun was effective up to a range of about seventy yards. Because of their versatility, these guns were very common among farmers and settlers on the frontier in 18th Century America. Many militia soldiers carried their personal fowling guns when they served in the American Revolution.

Frizzen – The part of a flintlock weapon that the flint strikes to make a spark and ignite the gunpowder.

Furlough – A period of time that the army occasionally granted to its soldiers. Furloughs were sometimes given when men were sick or wounded. Occasionally, during winter months, the army granted furloughs for men to return home so that the government did not have to house and feed them through the winter.

Gallows – Structures used for the execution of criminals by hanging.

Greatcoat – An outer coat, usually made of wool or linen. In order to be properly dressed, men were expected to wear such a coat when they went outside. It was ordinarily not buttoned in the front, so that the waistcoat could be seen beneath it. Sometimes the front was secured at the top with hooks, especially in military greatcoats.

Guardhouse – The jail inside a military facility.

Gunpowder – Also called "**powder**," this was an explosive compound that was used to fire weapons. Many men on the frontier carried their powder in hollowed out horns from cows called, "**powder horns**."

His Majesty – The proper, formal reference to the King of England. A queen is called, "Her Majesty."

Huzzah – A joyful shout, and the early form of the modern words "hoorah" and "hooray."

Indentured Servitude – This was a form of "voluntary slavery" in which poor people signed over their freedom to wealthy people for a set period of time. In return for their years of servitude they earned something such as passage by ship to America, the learning of a work trade, or shelter and food.

Indian – A traditional term used to refer to Native Americans. The term arose out of the confusion of early explorers. When they arrived in the Americas they thought that they had reached the east coast of India. Therefore, they referred to the native peoples as "Indians." The name "stuck" and became a word of common use in the United States.

Injun – The slang word for "Indian."

Lead – The soft metal used to make projectiles for rifles and muskets. It is still used to make modern projectiles.

Lean-to shelter – A simple, three-sided survival shelter. It is constructed by erecting two upright poles that support a longer horizontal pole. Then, limbs and branches are leaned at an angle on one side, normally in the direction that offers the most protection from the wind. Similar branches are added to the two narrow ends. Sometimes the back and sides of lean-tos were further protected against the rain with tarps or animal hides. The open side of the shelter normally faced a campfire.

Leggings – Also known as "**Gaiters**," these were protective garments for the lower legs. They were often made of wool, canvas, cotton, or animal skins. They were secured with buttons or straps and served to protect and insulate the exposed lower leg between the breeches and shoes.

Litter – A makeshift vehicle used to transport sick or wounded soldiers. Similar to a modern stretcher, it was often made of cloth or animal skins suspended between two poles. It could be carried by people on foot or dragged behind a horse.

Long Knives – Recorded also as **Big Knives**, this was the name given by the local Native Americans to the Virginia Army under Col. George Rogers Clark.

Loyalist – A citizen of the American colonies loyal to King George III and Great Britain.

Market Wallet – A long linen sack used for shopping. The market wallet was an enclosed sleeve, three to four feet in length, that had a foot-long slit opening in the center on one side. Shoppers placed their items in the opening and allowed them to settle at each end. The market wallet was carried over the shoulder, with the items dangling safely in front and over the back. They would squeeze the central opening closed with their hand to keep their items safe and prevent them from falling out of the sack. Soldiers also sometimes carried clothing and other items in a market wallet, thus using it as an improvised "suitcase" for travel.

Marsh Tacky - The **Carolina Marsh Tacky** or **Marsh Tacky** is a rare breed of horse native to South Carolina It is a member of the Colonial Spanish group of horse breeds. It is a small horse, well adapted for use in the lowland swamps of its native South Carolina. The Marsh Tacky developed from Spanish horses brought to the South Carolina coast by Spanish explorers, settlers and traders as early as the 16th century. The horses were used by the colonists during the American Revolution, and by South Carolinians for farm work, herding cattle and hunting throughout the breed's history.

Militia – Local county and state military units. Most served locally. There were both Patriot and Loyalist militia units during the war. French militia units served with either the British or American forces.

Moccasins – Typical lightweight footwear of the Eastern Woodland Indians. Made from animal hides, these shoes often had a thread that was pulled through the leather on top that caused it to have its distinguishing "pucker."

Muster – The official forming of local militia units for mobilization in the war.

Necessary House – This was the common name for an outhouse or outdoor toilet in the 18th Century.

Oath of Allegiance – This was a custom in the 1700's. Men would "swear their oath" to a nation, state, or king as a demonstration of their loyalty. Men who swore such oaths usually signed their names on official documents. In the Revolutionary War this was a demonstration of Patriotic Service either to England or to the United States.

Palisades – Walls made from upright stakes or tree trunks that were often pointed on top. They were built for defense, such as in the walls of primitive forts.

Parched Corn – Roasted grains of corn, similar to popcorn. Made by roasting kernels of corn in a dry pot or skillet, then adding salt to taste. Parched corn kept and traveled well and was a staple food for both natives and settlers on the frontier. It could be eaten alone as a snack or added to soups and stews.

Parley – Formal negotiations between opposing armies.

Patriots – People in American who were in favor of separation from England and the formation of a separate country.

Patrol – A military tactic which involved sending soldiers out into the countryside to scout for any presence of the enemy.

Queue – Pronounced "kew." This is the word for a man's ponytail. Men in Colonial times wore their hair long. They would often tie it in the back or braid it into a queue.

Redcoats – The derogatory name that Patriots called British soldiers.

Runner – Before the development of modern technology, messages had to be carried "on foot." Men or boys who delivered messages between a commander and the army were simply called "runners."

Scythe - A scythe is an agricultural hand tool for mowing grass or harvesting crops. It had a long, bowed handle. At the bottom there was a long, curved, sharp blade. Farm workers swung the razor-sharp blade so that they might cut tall grasses or grains at ground level. Swinging a scythe was difficult and exhausting work.

Sentry – A soldier who stands guard at a military encampment or facility, or along a roadway. Armies placed sentries on duty any time they wanted to keep an eye out for enemy soldiers or suspicious activity.

Shooting Pouch – A leather bag worn by frontiersmen. They carried their ammunition and tools for taking care of their musket or rifle in the pouch.

Siege – A military tactic in which an army surrounds another army, usually confined in a town or fort. Once the enemy army is contained, the army laying siege bombards them with fire until the army under siege calls for a surrender.

Spectacles – The historic name for eyeglasses.

Spit – A metal or wooden rod that is used for roasting meat over an open fire. The rod is inserted through the length of an animal or large piece of meat then the ends of the spit are suspended on upright poles, thus allowing the meat to hang over the center of the fire. A spit also provides the cook the ability to rotate the meat and, thus, cook it evenly on all sides.

Spyglass – A small handheld telescope used for observing at a distance. Spyglasses predated binoculars.

They were used by men at sea, as well as by explorers and military commanders in the field.

Station – Another name for a frontier fort.

Surgeon – A military doctor. The practice of medicine was quite different during the Colonial period. There were not many medical schools or universities. Many doctors learned "on the job" from other doctors. Military surgeons spent most of their time treating battle wounds and the various diseases that afflicted their armies.

Surrender – The formal, official end of a military conflict when one army acknowledges that the other is victor. Surrender often has certain terms to which both parties in the negotiation must agree.

Tankard – A large, cylindrical drinking cup with a single handle. Often made of wood, pewter, brass, or tin.

Tomahawk – A bladed weapon that resembled an axe or hatchet. This useful tool was used both in combat as well as in camp life.

Tory / Tories – Another name for Loyalists.

Turn Coat – (Verb) To abandon or desert one side in a cause or argument and then join the opposing side. The phrase is an ancient one. Almost 1,000 years ago, it described changing allegiances from one lord or king to another ... literally turning from one coat of arms to another. Later, in military history, it described turning one's topcoat inside-out, thus revealing the lining of the coat (usually a different color) and displaying one's turning from the colors of the army.

Turncoat – (Noun) One who shifts their loyalty or allegiance from one cause to another. The word often carries a negative meaning. Calling one a "turncoat" would be considered an insult when used by people whose cause had been abandoned. Example: *"You no longer serve England or her King. You are nothing but a lousy turncoat!"*

Wax Seal – People usually sealed their private letters with a melted blob of hot wax and then pressed a piece of metal into the wax to make an impression or "seal." This was a way to ensure that private letters were not opened until they reached their destination.

Weskit – Also known as a **waistcoat**, this was the vest worn over the top of a man's shirt and under a man's coat. It would sometimes be worn without the outer overcoat. It was a more formal outer garment.

Wet Nurse – A woman who served as a substitute to nurse a baby when the baby's mother could not do so. Often, when something tragic happened to the mother of a newborn, the family would seek out and hire a wet nurse to feed the baby until it was ready to eat solid food.

Whigs – Also known as Patriots, Revolutionaries, Continentals, or Rebels. They were residents of the thirteen colonies who rejected British rule and declared independence from Great Britain in July 1776.

A MESSAGE FROM THE AUTHOR

Thank you for reading my story!

I hope that you enjoyed my work of fiction. It was a pleasure preparing and writing it for you. I am just a simple "part-time" author, and I am humbled that you chose to read my book.

I would humbly ask that you help me spread the word about my historical fiction books for kids. You can help me in a number of ways!

•**Tell your friends!** Word of mouth is always the best!

•**Mention my books on Facebook or in other social media.** I know lots of students use social media these days. Please mention me, or maybe even post a picture of you reading one of my books!

•**Get your parents to write a review for me on Amazon.com.** Reviews are so very important. They help other readers discover good books. Tell your parents what you thought about the book and ask them to put your words into the review.

•**Connect with me and like my author page on Face-**

book @cockedhatpublishing, and follow me on Twitter @GeoffBaggett.

•**Tell your teachers about me!** I have a unique and interesting Revolutionary War presentation available for elementary and middle school classes. I actually bring a trunk full of items from the American Revolution and provide a "hands-on" experience for students. I even dress up couple of volunteers in replica Revolutionary War militia uniforms! I am a professional speaker and living historian, and I absolutely love to travel and visit in schools. Get your teachers to contact me through my web site, geoffbaggett.com, or through my Facebook author page, to arrange an event.

Thanks again! And remember to tell all of your friends about the *Patriot Kids of the American Revolution Series*!

Geoff Baggett

ABOUT THE AUTHOR

Geoff Baggett is a historical researcher and author with a passion for all things Revolutionary War. He is an active member of the Sons of the American Revolution and the Descendants of Washington's Army at Valley Forge.

Geoff has discovered over twenty American Patriot ancestors in his family tree. He is an avid living historian, appearing regularly in period clothing and uniforms in classrooms, reenactments, and other commemorative events. He lives with his family on a quiet little place in the country in rural western Kentucky.

OTHER BOOKS FOR YOUNG READERS
BY GEOFF BAGGETT

Patriot Kids of the American Revolution Series

Book 1 - Little Hornet

Book 2 - Little Warrior

Book 3 - Little Spy of Vincennes

Book 4 - Little Brother

Book 5 - Little Camp Follower

Book 6 - Little Turncoat

Kentucky Frontier Adventures

Book 1 - A Bucket Full of Courage

Betsy Johnson of Bryan Station

Book 2 - Always Looking For a Home

The Sons of Squire Boone

My Colonial Journal for Boys

My Colonial Journal for Girls